Love's Belief

Wartime Brides, Book 3

By Linda Shenton

Matchett

Love's Belief

By Linda Shenton Matchett

To the men and women

who risked their lives

to fight evil

Chapter One

"I thought *Frau* Schmidt was going to die." Pia Hertz blew out a deep breath. "We haven't had a difficult birth like that in a long time, *Mutti.*"

"*Ja,* but you are a gifted midwife, Pia. I wasn't too worried."

Pia chuckled. "You always say that."

Mutti linked her arm with Pia's. "We must have confidence, otherwise fear will make us prone to mistakes. Now, let's reward ourselves with strudel, if we can find it, hmm?"

"A wonderful idea. I'm starving. Hopefully, the baker has some, and the line won't be too long at this early hour. Selections at most of the shops have been meager as the war has ground on."

Leaning close to Pia's ear, *Mutti* whispered, "Be careful what you say. You don't want to be accused of sedition."

Pia cast a glance over her shoulder. "You're right. It doesn't seem to take much to get arrested these days." She sighed. "I don't understand why God has allowed *Herr* Hitler to succeed. Why has He not stepped in to save His people, the Jews?"

Dust coated their shoes as they sauntered along the sidewalk, skirting the piles of rubble from the most recent RAF bombing raid.

"There are some things we will never have an answer to, Daughter, but we must trust in His plan. It is difficult. Despite being a believer since childhood, I still struggle with doubts. It's understandable that you do, too." She stroked Pia's cheek. "When we get home, let's pray together and see what He would have us do."

Pia stifled a gasp. "What are you suggesting?"

Her lips pressed in a thin line, *Mutti* frowned. She jerked her head toward the SS officer standing about ten meters away, then tugged on Pia's arm. Continuing down the sidewalk, they arrived at the bakery. Unlit windows and lack of women waiting indicated there were no more treats to be had for the day.

"*Ach,* we'll have to assuage our penchant for a sweet another time." *Mutti* rubbed her belly. "Let's take a shortcut down *Rosenstrasse* then head for the river. It would be nice to look at something other than damaged buildings and debris."

"Good idea. It is warmer today than yesterday, and there is a market at the end of the street. Perhaps they have some bread or cheese we can nibble on."

A chill swept over Pia as they walked past a Vichy police officer, their eyes averted to avoid any interaction. An elderly couple tottered along in front of them, holding hands and speaking softly. Pia's heart tugged. Would she ever find someone to spend her life with: someone to look at her like the wrinkled, gray-haired man gazed at the petite woman by his side? At twenty-eight, it seemed unlikely. *Der Führer's* desire to rule the world was destroying an entire generation of young men, and she certainly had no interest in a black-coated member of the SS.

Her grip tightened on *Mutti's* arm, and she frowned. Would this war never end?

The distant hum of voices wafted toward her and urged *Mutti* to increase her pace. Moments later, they turned the corner onto *Rosenstrasse* and froze. Gathered in front of one of the factories, a group of several hundred women raised their fists and chanted, "Give us our husbands back."

Dozens of armed guards surrounded the mob. Intermittent commands of "Clear the street or we'll shoot" peppered the air. Some of the protestors scattered, but many held their ground.

Pia's gaze whipped toward *Mutti*, who froze, her face ashen and mouth agape. She turned her terror-filled eyes to Pia. "What are they doing? They will be arrested and sent away, never to be seen again. We must go. We can't let the authorities think we are part of this." She tugged on Pia's hands.

"Wait. I want to find out what is happening." She pointed to a small group of men and women huddled some distance away, arms crossed and talking among themselves. "Those people aren't involved, but maybe they know what's going on."

"Please hurry, Pia. We cannot risk going to jail…or worse." *Mutti's* lips trembled. "Could this day get any worse?"

"I'm sorry, *Mutti*. You're right. We should go." She turned toward *Rochstrasse*.

"No, it is me who should apologize. I am a foolish old woman. Talk to those people. We need to know what's going on. We cannot bury our heads in the rubble."

"Are you sure?" Pia searched *Mutti's* face.

"*Ja.* We cannot count on the incident being in the newspapers. The authorities may not want the public to know about this."

With a curt nod, Pia edged around the throng and approached the group bunched together away from the demonstrators. "I am Pia Hertz. Do you know what is happening?"

A ginger-haired woman whose ragged clothing hung on her gaunt frame nodded. "There has been a mass arrest of Jews who are married to non-Jews." Her lips twisted. "Apparently, the Gestapo have changed their minds about the people they want to clear out of Berlin. Yesterday, they stormed the factories and arrested every Jew inside, even those previously exempted. All over the city, men have been dragged from their homes."

Eyes glistening with tears, a middle-aged man spat on the ground. "I saw two SS soldiers grab a girl who was wearing the star and shove her into a truck. They were very rough with her. I could hear her crying. What kind of men do that?"

Dressed in a mismatched blouse and skirt, a wizened, old woman wiped tears from her eyes. "I heard they are all being locked up in the administrative center of the Jewish community and are certain to be deported to one of the camps."

Pia glanced back at the protestors. "Aren't those women afraid of being arrested?"

She shrugged. "Maybe they don't care. If my husband was taken, I would do whatever it took to get him released. Wouldn't you?"

"I'm not married." Pia's face warmed. Even strangers assumed she should be married by now.

"Is your sweetheart serving in one of the armed forces?"

"I don't have a boyfriend." Pia ducked her head. "Thank you for the information. I must take my mother home."

"Of course." The old man gestured toward *Rochstrasse* and smirked. "Go that way, so you don't have to pass by the demonstrators. I imagine Goebbels doesn't want a publicity nightmare by killing a bunch of women, but who knows if one of these soldiers has an itchy finger. Tempers are high. It won't take much to light the match."

With a nod, she pulled her skirts closer to her legs and hastened to where she'd left her mother. Pia wrapped her arm around *Mutti's* shoulder. "Let's go. I'll explain on the way."

They pivoted away from the mob, and Pia rammed into a tall, bearded man about her own age. He dropped the box he balanced in one hand, and her fingers closed over the empty, left sleeve of his coat to steady herself. Unbalanced, she crumpled to the ground and landed on her backside with an unladylike grunt.

Face red to the roots of his close-cropped dark hair, he bent and helped her climb to her feet. Concern darkened his crystal-blue eyes. "Are you okay? My apologies for running into you."

"*Ja.* I'm fine. It was my fault. I was in a hurry and didn't see you." She looked at their hands, still intertwined, and a nervous giggle escaped.

He snatched away his hand and jammed it into his pocket. With a slight bow, he scrutinized her face. "If you're sure you're not hurt—"

"I'm sure. Thank you for your assistance." Her fingers tingled from the contact of his warm grip as she wiped gray dust from her clothes. Pia's breath hitched, and she nibbled the inside of her lip. What was wrong with her? At the first interaction in months with a handsome man under the age of eighty she was acting like a schoolgirl. "Come, *Mutti*. We don't want to be late."

"Late? We're not—"

"Thank you again." Pia dipped her head at the stranger and nudged her mother forward.

"Good day." The man stepped to the side and winked. "And watch where you are going. You don't want to ruin that pretty outfit. New dresses are hard to come by these days."

She glanced down at her worn, but serviceable outfit. What did he know of acquiring women's clothing? Was he mocking her? A frown began to form, then she caught sight of the twinkle in his eyes. He bowed again, picked up his box, and headed in the direction of the demonstration.

Watching his departing figure, she heard her mother snicker. She turned and straightened her spine. "What?"

Merriment had smoothed away the stress from *Mutti's* face. "It's been a long time since I have seen you blush in the presence of a man. Perhaps we should find out who he is."

Pia rolled her eyes. "Nonsense. I was embarrassed about my fall, nothing more. Besides, he's disappeared into the crowd. I've no inclination to search for him."

"Your mouth says one thing, but your face another."

"We're wasting time. Let's be on our way." Pia shook her head in a futile effort to rid herself of the man's image: his firm jaw emphasized by the well-groomed goatee and sky-blue eyes that seem to change colors with his mood. What would it be like to have that gaze focused on her every day?

Love's Belief 8

Chapter Two

Dieter Fertig stifled the impulse to glance back at the spunky young woman with the chocolate-brown eyes. She'd seemed more agitated by the older woman's disagreement about being tardy than falling at his feet in a heap. He chuckled at the look of irritation that shot sparks from her eyes. She'd stiffened when he teased her about her dress, then a tentative smile transformed her lovely face into a glow like the noonday sun.

Had she been part of the protest? Did she have a Jewish husband? He scrubbed at his face with cold fingers. What did he care? He'd never see her again. And even if he did, what woman in her right mind would be interested in him, a maimed ex-soldier who often awoke drenched in sweat from nightmares?

He hunched into his coat and tucked the delivery under the stump of his left arm. Good thing the package only contained nonbreakable items. Despite her petite frame, the young woman had hit him with such force, the box had sailed from his hand and landed with a thud on the pavement. He'd wait until arriving at his destination to check the contents.

The chaos from the protest continued, with women hurling insults and accusations at the guards. He crossed the street as the crowd continued to swell in number, with few men in attendance. Most were either in uniform or working in some segment of Hitler's war machine. Others like

Love's Belief 9

him, merchants who ran small shops, or the elderly and infirm, typically tried to stay out of view.

A clock on a nearby church struck the hour, but he remained mesmerized by the stalwart women who refused to back down, even in the face of armed guards. Would he ever have someone he could share his life with again who would fight for him like these ladies? Unlikely. He'd spend the rest of his days selling bits and pieces to the public.

The breeze kicked up, and he shivered. Dust swirled on the pavement. Tucking his scarf closer to his neck, he studied the expressions of the protestors. Grief-stricken faces intermingled among those etched with anger. Others communicated confusion or dread. This was the third day of the protest. Would it end in tragedy or victory? Or both?

With an eye on the soldiers, Dieter tramped down the sidewalk. Jostled by new arrivals, he cast a glance toward the shouting throng and froze. A young woman with flowing, raven-colored hair and spectacles raised her fist to the air, her voice blending with the crowd. Was that Lar's wife, Valma?

He rose on his toes and craned his neck. The group surged forward, and the woman disappeared among the others. Should he call out to her? A cadre of guards strode through the mob, and the woman came into view. She turned, her bulging stomach heralding an impending birth. Her unmistakable profile that held a strawberry birthmark on her cheek was the impetus he needed.

A quick peek to the left and right indicated the clear roadway, so he trotted in her direction. Why was she participating in the demonstration? Was Lars Jewish? The couple were members of the Lutheran church he attended, so it seemed unlikely. Perhaps she was supporting a friend. If so, she was very brave. The Gestapo did not take kindly to opposition.

His step hitched. Lars would be distraught if he discovered his wife was here. Now that Dieter knew, he couldn't withhold the information from his friend. Hopefully, he could persuade her to leave before she came to any harm.

Threading his way through the crush of bodies, he made his way to Valma's side. He leaned close to her ear. "Valma, why are you here? It's not safe. Come with me, and I'll escort you home."

Her head whipped around, her eyes wide, and perspiration beaded along her hairline despite the cold. "What?"

"You shouldn't be in this crowd. It's dangerous. You could fall or be trampled. Or worse, arrested. Does Lars know you're here?"

Fear clouded her eyes. Tears coursed down her cheeks. "He was taken the day before yesterday with about two thousand other Jews who are married to what they are calling *Aryan* Germans." Her voice was colored with anger.

Dieter gaped at her, his mind racing. "Lars is Jewish?"

"Who are they to say we can't be together. Hitler has gone too far, and we must dissent. The madness needs to be stopped. I'm not leaving until my husband has been released." She stroked her swollen abdomen. "Lars should be home for the birth of his child."

He gripped her arm and jerked his head toward a clear patch of sidewalk. "I can barely hear you with this noise. Please, follow me and tell me what happened."

Valma hesitated for a moment, then gave a curt nod. "But only for a few moments. The authorities must not think we are giving up." She trailed him to the open space.

An empty planter stood near a small ash tree. He lowered her onto the edge. "Rest."

She sighed, a grateful smile on her lips.

Dropping next to her, he said, "I didn't know Lars was Jewish. How did the Gestapo find out?"

A half-hearted shrug lifted her shoulders. "How do they ferret out all they do? And yes, he is Jewish. His great-grandmother was a Jew from Poland. Lars told me about her when we first began courting several years ago. He saw the signs and didn't want me to be surprised if something came of the information. I didn't care about that. No one should care about that." Her bottom lip trembled. "Anyway, we thought he'd be safe when the laws said that Jews married to non-Jews were exempt. We were fools."

Leaning toward her, he wrapped his arm around her shoulder. He shook his head. "No, you believed Hitler like we all did. We're only just now finding out how despicable he is. The only question is whether the Allies will defeat him before he rids Germany of the majority of her people."

Her eyes widened. "Lower your voice. Saying things like that will get you arrested…or worse."

"Nothing can be worse than what I experienced on the battle lines. Bombs and bullets killing and maiming everything in their path. Men screaming in agony. The skies filled with smoke and chemicals choking the air from our lungs." Memories pelted his mind, and he shuddered.

Phantom pain bit into his stump. "I have seen the worst man has to offer. They cannot scare me, but you are a woman. You should be home safe, not risking your life. What can yelling at the Gestapo do?"

"Maybe nothing, but I won't go down without a fight. Lars would do the same for me. I can do no less." She crossed her arms and propped them on her large belly. "Do you really think the guards would shoot a bunch of women, some of whom are pregnant?"

"I don't know what to think anymore." He blew out a deep breath and observed the pandemonium.

She nudged his shoulder. "Besides, this is the third day. We seem to be wearing them down."

Squinting, he studied the guards' faces. Some of them did appear to be uncertain. Or was it fatigue? "Lars has been my friend since we were in short pants. How could I not realize his family was Jewish? What else don't I know, Valma? How should I respond to all of this? I did my part for Germany, and the *Vaterland* repaid me by arresting my best friend."

"And my husband. Stay. Join the protest. You said it yourself. What else can they do to you?"

"I can't. I'm already late delivering to the Eckhardts. They will worry, and then Mr. Eckhardt might decide to come find me. That would be bad. His health is declining, and this weather would not be good for him." He gazed into her eyes. "Are you sure you shouldn't take a break for a bit?"

"No, but we won't remain much longer. The women tend to disperse around dinnertime and then come back each morning after they've seen their children off to school. My friend, Gerta, will walk me home. We live in the same building." She rose and hugged him. "You have work to do. Don't waste more time. But pray for us, Dieter. Pray that this nightmare ends, and they release our husbands."

He nodded then frowned as she turned and hurried toward the ever-growing horde. Climbing to his feet, he did as she asked. *Dear Father God, please allow these men to be freed to return to their families. Keep Valma safe. My heart is broken that Germany has turned away from You and is persecuting many of its citizens. These women are braver than I have been, by standing up for what they believe in. I can no longer hide from responsibility. Please show me what You would have me do, even if it means losing my life in the process.*

Chapter Three

Pia yawned as she shifted the canvas satchel on her shoulder. It had been another long night delivering a baby, but if she didn't get to the market early, there'd be nothing remaining on the shelves. She yanked open the door to the shop located a few blocks from home. The tiny store was packed with women of all ages, grasping and shoving to fill their bags with food items.

Behind the wooden counter, her friend Trudy sat on a stool, a look of contentment on her face despite the mayhem. Her arms rested on her protruding belly, the most likely reason for the aura of peace surrounding her.

Outside, the muffled sound of marching feet rumbled on the pavement. Pia turned toward the noise. Dozens of *Hitlerjugend* paraded past the window, heads tipped to the sky, their expressions haughty. One of the young men carried the organization's flag, the swastika stark against red and white bands. She shuddered. Teenage boys should be playing Cat and Mouse or cycling, not performing military drills. Initially recruiting boys with hiking and camping trips, the group no longer had to tantalize them to join after membership became mandatory in 1936.

Thank you God that I don't have any brothers to be forced into following tenets we do not believe.

"*Guten Morgen*, Pia." Trudy lifted her hand in greeting. "You look tired. A baby last night?"

Ja. Frau Zimmerman had twin girls. That makes six. *Herr* Zimmerman was ecstatic. I would have thought he'd want a boy." She shrugged. "But he gave me several coins above my regular fee and grinned like a child at the circus."

"There's no accounting for what people want." Trudy gestured to the shelves. "Before the war, our patrons were somewhat finicky. Now, they are glad to find something edible. Perhaps *Herr* Zimmerman is simply happy to have a healthy child."

"You're right. I shouldn't be so cynical." Pia leaned over the counter. "But it's getting harder to maintain the joy. How many more young men must die for a madman? And how many more of our Jewish friends must be arrested?"

"Shh!" Trudy frowned. "You know saying such things could get *you* arrested. Be careful. The shop is full, and who knows if anyone is related to the Gestapo."

Pia blew out a loud breath. "You're right. It must be my fatigue talking."

"Perhaps the tide is turning. Remember, the *Rosenstrasse* protest was successful. The men were released, and no one was injured."

"It's been two weeks, and from what I've heard, most of those who were freed went into hiding. Even they don't believe they are safe." She rubbed her forehead. "Enough. I am depressing myself, and this sort of negativity isn't good for your baby. How are you feeling? With only four weeks to go, you must be getting excited."

"And scared, too. I'm not sure what to expect other than pain. Will it be terrible?"

"Labor is different for each woman, but you'll do fine. Don't worry. *Mutti* and I will both attend the birth."

Trudy squeezed Pia's hand. "Then all will be well. Now, go get your groceries before there is nothing on the shelves."

Pia snorted a laugh. "So much for *Der Führer's* Four Year Plan. It worked only until we were at war." She pivoted and made her way through the aisles, snatching cans and produce with little thought. *Mutti* would figure out what to cook with whatever Pia brought home.

Customers made their purchases and cleared the shop. Soon, Pia was alone. The bell over the door jangled, and she looked up. Smiling, she hurried to the petite blonde woman who entered, her hand resting protectively around her middle. Six months with child, Bruni Bachman wore pregnancy well, and the joy of motherhood shone on her face. Her silk suit rustled under her wool coat as she walked, her leather shoes whispering against the floor. Her father must still be providing for Bruni and Erich.

"Bruni, how lovely to see you. Feeling better, I see."

"Yes, the morning sickness seems to have passed. Thank goodness. Erich was beginning to worry, even though you told me it was normal."

"He is a first-time father. He'll get used to it."

Bruni giggled. "*Nein.* He gets squeamish with a paper cut. And *Vati* is treating me like a porcelain doll. Ever since *Mutti* passed away, he barely lets me go anywhere alone." She gestured to the sleek, cream-colored Mercedes-Benz coupe parked along the street where her father sat, stone-faced. He insists that his chauffeur drive me everywhere. It's a bit embarrassing, really."

A glance outside, and Pia gulped at the sight of her patient's formidable father, *Herr* Noll. "He accompanied you today?"

"He has some sort of important meeting with Count von Krosigk, and the shop is on the way."

"Von Krosigk? Isn't he the minister of finance?"

"Something like that. Why?"

"Nothing. With your father being a banker, I shouldn't be surprised, but I wasn't aware he was so well connected."

"*Vati* has all kinds of men in suits coming and going. It's rather tedious actually, because I'm required to remain out of sight when he has visitors. With Erich working long hours, I'm by myself quite a bit."

"I didn't realize you still lived with your parents."

"We just moved back. *Vati* didn't want me to be alone while Erich was at the factory."

"Of course. That makes sense." Pia nibbled her lower lip. Was Bruni's father a Nazi, or was he simply a well-placed businessman? His piercing gaze never seemed to miss anything, and as a man of few words, it was difficult to know what he thought. Just because he seemed foreboding, didn't mean he was an evil man, did it?

Pia stroked the rough sleeve of Bruni's coat. "This is lovely. Is it new?"

Bruni's face pinked, and she nodded. "*Vati* gave it to me when we found out I was pregnant. He said my cape was not sufficient to keep out the chill. I could hardly say no, although Erich was upset. He wants to be the one to provide for me, but until he gets seniority at work, his salary won't cover extras like this."

"I haven't seen coats in the shops since last winter." Pia cocked her head. "Where on earth did he find such an item?"

"I don't know. Perhaps from France. It is a Dior." She patted her flawless chignon. "I'm sorry to rush off, but I can't keep *Vati* waiting. I will see you next month at my appointment." She withdrew a card from her purse and handed it to Pia. "Here is the address. I should have told you about the move, but with everything going on, it completely slipped my mind. Forgive me."

"Absolutely. I'm glad you'll be looked after."

Moments later, Bruni purchased her items and waved as she left the shop, her floral perfume lingering in the air.

Pia dumped the contents of her bag on the counter, and Trudy began to tally her prices. A crease appeared between her brows, and she whispered to herself as she added the column. She placed the items back into the bag, and handed Pia the receipt.

Rummaging in her purse, Pia dug out the appropriate coins and pressed them into Trudy's hand. She whispered, "Are we the only ones in the shop?"

"Yes, why?"

"Do you think Bruni's father is a Nazi?"

Trudy's eyes widened, and her face paled. "I…I don't know. Why do you ask?"

"He's meeting with the minister of finance. Is he providing money to the war machine? Or perhaps doing more?"

"It's not for us to speculate. Not if you want to stay out of trouble."

"What if Bruni is a Nazi?"

"Now you're being ridiculous. What could Bruni do for the war machine, as you call it? And why the sudden interest? You deliver babies, something positive in these dark days. Keep busy with that, and you won't have time to worry about other things."

"You're right, but I can't help but feel there must be something I can do to alleviate the suffering, especially of the Jews. I don't have a husband, so I can't fully understand the terror of those women whose husbands were arrested, but I know it must have been awful. What would you have done if it had been your husband?"

Trudy kneaded her hands, but remained mute.

"The laws are getting worse. It won't be long before it's not safe for anyone. Ever since the protest, *Mutti* and I have been praying for how God wants us to respond."

Trudy narrowed her eyes. "If you are committed about being involved, I know someone, but it won't be easy, and it will be dangerous."

Chapter Four

Static crackled from the tiny radio on the shelf behind the counter in Dieter's shop. He twisted the knob in an attempt to clear the noise. Tonight's *Wunschkonzert* program was supposed to feature Lala Andersen performing her famous love song "Lili Marlene."

He smirked. Rumor was that her velvet tones made the song so popular even Allied soldiers listened to it. Goebbels had issued the order to cease broadcasting it, but months later the mandate was rescinded. Another rumor claimed it was Rommel's favorite tune. Perhaps the reason behind the action. There seemed to be no end to the machinations of the Nazi leadership.

Pops and hisses continued to emit from the wireless, but no amount of fiddling improved the sound quality. Hopefully he would be able to hear the music when the program started this evening. He'd hate to miss the variety of pop songs, instrumental marches, and comic sketches. One or two of his favorite stars usually made an appearance.

With church in the morning and the *Wunschkonzert* at night, he was almost able to escape the harsh realities of war on Sundays. Dieter sighed and walked to the display case at the front of the store and began to inventory his few unsold products. Back to the real world of shortages and deprivation.

Time passed quickly as he made his way around the shop noting his remaining stock. Movement outside the window caught his eye, and he looked up. Bundled in multiple layers with blankets covering their shoulders, *Herr* and *Frau* Waller waved at him through the dust-coated panes. Smiles lit up the wrinkled faces of the elderly couple who lived across the street. They motioned for him to join them.

He unlocked the door and stepped outside. A frigid blast of air enveloped him, and he shivered. "Come inside."

Frau Waller shook her head and pressed a warm, towel-wrapped parcel into his hand. "We cannot stay. Here is fresh bread. Take it. You are too thin."

"How did you—"

"Our son has come to take us to live with him in Dresden. He thinks we'll be safer. There is little room for supplies in the car, so I baked several loaves of bread for those who have been kind to us."

"I didn't do much. Give this to someone truly in need."

"We've taken care of many already, and this is the last loaf. Please...take it." Tears trickled down *Frau* Waller's cheeks. "It is only a small token, but we wanted you to know how much your friendship has meant to us. Who knows how long this war will go on...or whether we will ever come back to Berlin."

"*Danke*. I will miss you. With my own parents gone..." He swallowed past the growing lump in his throat. "Your friendship is important to me also. Godspeed." He nestled the bread under his stump and hugged them with his other arm.

"God has a special plan in mind for you." *Herr* Waller whispered into his ear. "We'll pray you determine what it is."

"What?" Dieter jerked back.

"*Herr* Waller tucked his wife's hand through his elbow and waved. "*Auf Wiedersehen.*" The couple hunched together against the wind and toddled across the street to their home.

Icy needles clawed at Dieter's face, and he rushed into the shop, slamming the door behind him. He turned the lock and placed the loaf on the counter. Blowing on his fingers, he hopped around trying to warm up.

"What did *Herr* and *Frau* Waller know about God's plans for him? Had God actually spoken to them? He shook his head. Ridiculous. Why would God speak to them, but not him?

He wanted to do something to ease the suffering of those impacted by the war, but it seemed unlikely a one-armed veteran with little to his name could make a difference. His stomach rumbled, and he uncovered the fragrant bread. Tearing off a corner, he popped it into his mouth and moaned. How long had it been since he'd had anything so flavorful?

"Thank You God for the Wallers and for their friendship. Please protect them as they travel. Help them adjust to moving from their home where they have lived for so very long." He tore off another piece from the loaf. "And thanks for this gift of fresh bread." He covered up the food and sighed. Was it truly wise to relocate to the ancient city? Dresden had several military facilities including the *Albertstadt* garrison.

A knock sounded.

Dieter rushed to unlock the door and pulled it open to his friend Gerhard Cotta. So much for getting any work done. "*Wie Gehts?* What are you doing out on such a cold afternoon? You should be home in front of the stove."

Gerhard clapped him on the shoulder and laughed before shutting the door. "You mean my stove that is as cold as Hitler's heart? I ran out of coal two days ago."

"Don't say such things. You could be arrested. Didn't you hear about that doctor who poked fun at Göring and was never seen again?"

"Bah. There is no one to hear me."

Dieter shook his head. "I wouldn't put anything past the Gestapo. And the *Blockwarts* are everywhere, party members watching for someone to make a mistake or break some miniscule law no one has heard of."

"Now who is saying things they shouldn't?" Gerhard lifted his nose and sniffed. "Is that bread I smell? Where did you get it?"

Dieter gestured to the towel-wrapped loaf. "Help yourself. *Frau* Waller brought it. Their son is moving them south for their safety."

"Is anywhere in Germany safe? The Allies have become bolder with their bombing. In the past, their RAF had not done much damage, but they seem to have developed something that makes them more precise, more deadly."

"Probably not. From within or from without."

"There you go again making seditious statements. What's gotten into you today, Dieter? Did something happen?"

Dieter blew out a heavy breath. "Not recently, but I can't get those women who protested on *Rosenstrasse* out of my mind. They stood up for what they believed in and were able to make a difference. Small, perhaps, but an impact nonetheless." He paced in front of the window, his boots clomping against the wooden floor. "What am I doing? Running a shop." He pointed at one of the sparse shelves. "And for how much longer? It's getting harder to acquire foodstuffs and other necessities."

"You did your part for the war and gave a piece of yourself in the process. You have nothing to be ashamed of."

"I'm not ashamed. Not really. God knows, I don't want to keep this war going by fighting for a cause I disagree with…perpetuating the evil. But I am a mere merchant in a small shop; what can I do to draw attention to or alleviate the atrocities?" He stopped walking and stared out the window, his fingers massaging the ache in his stump.

Silence filled the tiny room, and seconds later Dieter turned toward Gerhard who stared at him with narrowed eyes. "I've said too much, Gerhard. I shouldn't put you in the position of having to deny hearing me talk like this. Forgive me. My heart is heavy today. I hate losing the Wallers' companionship."

"They've been like your *Mutti* and *Vati*, haven't they?"

"Yes, but there's more." Dieter hesitated, then plunged in. "Before he left, *Herr* Waller said something rather disturbing. He told me God has a special plan for me. What could he mean? How can God use me?" He raised his maimed arm. "I'm half the man I used to be."

Gerhard rose and strode toward him, his face dark. "Don't ever say that again. Just because you lost part of your arm, doesn't make you less of a man. And with your integrity and faith, you are more of a man than most others I know." He gripped Dieter's shoulders. "Besides, God uses unlikely characters, don't you know? Some believe Moses had a stutter. And what about Paul? He persecuted and killed Christians before God called him. Should God choose you, He will equip you to complete the task."

Dieter's heart lifted, and he chuckled. "When did you become a preacher?"

"Never, but perhaps *Herr* Waller is a prophet." Gerhard crossed his arms. "I came here today with a proposition, and I wasn't sure how to approach you. However, you've managed to open that door." He cleared his throat. "I love you like a brother and am hesitant to put you in danger, but we need you."

"We?"

Gerhard nodded. "I am part of a resistance cell which has been spiriting Jews out of the city. One of our transport people was arrested yesterday, and I was asked if I knew anyone who could do the job." He raised his gaze and looked deep into Dieter's eyes. "I thought of you immediately. You have a delivery truck."

"And no fuel."

"We can solve that problem."

A chill swept over Dieter. *Is this Your plan, God?*

Chapter Five

The metal mail slot in the front door clanged as a battered envelope fluttered to the floor and landed face up. The Nazi party's swastika encircled in black dominated the correspondence. Pia forced herself to breathe as she bent and retrieved the letter with trembling fingers.

What had she and *Mutti* done to gain the attention of the authorities? As mandated, they'd joined the midwives association and attended monthly meetings. Pia ran her fingers across the sealed envelope. The midwives assemblies touted the Nazi's support of their industry after years of neglect, but they also railed incessantly against the Jews. Would the authorities ask midwives to spy on families to make sure they were proper Aryan homes?

She held the missive to the light. Nothing. Hitler desired to increase the birth rates of ethnic Germans. A recent newspaper article hailed mother and child as the nation's most valuable treasures and declared midwifery to be the most noble and genuine female profession. A nice thought since midwife training had been improved and regulated, but the courses were held at the Alt-Rehse, a Nazi leader school. Pia shook her head and tapped the letter on her palm.

Perhaps she could pretend it hadn't arrived.

Her chest tight, she ran her finger under the flap before she could change her mind. She pulled out the crisp, high-quality stationery and unfolded it. Her gaze raced to the bottom of the letter, and she stared at the signature of Nanna Conti, head of the midwives organization for Germany.

Mrs. Conti and her son, the Reich health leader, were well-known for their virulent anti-Semitic beliefs. Pia shuddered at the woman's last recommendation that all midwives obtain the recently revised textbook filled with pejorative descriptions of Jews, blacks, and other nonwhite so-called undesirables. How could medical professionals only care for a portion of humankind and seek to harm the rest?

As footsteps sounded on the stairs, and Pia scanned the contents of the page. *Mutti* descended, concern wrinkling her forehead. "Is everything all right, Pia? You're white as salt."

Pia extended the letter to *Mutti* who clutched it in one hand, her frown deepening as she read.

She blanched, and her arm dropped. "This is serious. I wonder if all midwives received this or if we're being singled out because we're Christians and disagree with her leadership? Or is this another scare tactic the Nazis are using to ensure compliance?"

"It worked. I'm terrified, *Mutti*."

"Okay, let's think this through. Even though the envelope is addressed to us personally, the letter doesn't contain a salutation. Perhaps we should take it at face value as the reminder it claims to be, admonishing us to report all miscarriages, newborns with disabilities, ill babies, and children born of Jewish parents."

Pointing to the page, she quoted, "'Midwives are to teach mothers to be proud of fulfilling their duty toward the German nation, encouraging them to give birth to as many children as possible.' Tsk, tsk. Difficult to do when *der Führer* has relegated our young men to the front lines of battle."

"I wonder what other midwives think of this. How many do you think comply with these laws?" Pia rubbed her arms to ward off a chill. "Is anti-Semitism as rampant as this letter makes me think?"

"I doubt it, although it is running high and splitting families and friends. These laws are polarizing. One is either for them or against them, no middle ground. I'm glad you are with me, daughter. With God's help, we can fight this together. Let us pray for guidance." She grasped Pia's hands and led her to the worn, green sofa in front of their fireplace. The meager collection of coal nestled inside struggled to emit heat.

The strength of her mother's calloused grip gave testament to years of hard work. Pia smiled. Yes, they were only two women who delivered babies, but *Mutti's* faith buoyed her own. A sigh escaped, and the constriction eased around her chest.

Knee to knee, they sat with heads bowed. *Mutti's* voice broke the stillness. "Dear Father God, we don't know why You have allowed this evil to continue or what Your plans are for the future, but we are resting in the knowledge that You are in control. We are frightened about receiving this letter, that perhaps we are being scrutinized. We want to do Your will as we help mothers birth their children." She cleared her throat. "Most importantly, we want to save the babies the Nazis are trying to destroy. We don't know how, so please guide us and give us the means to do so. Please keep us safe in our mission. In Jesus' name. Amen."

Her eyes wide, Pia looked at *Mutti*. Her mother had just asked God's blessing on breaking the law. Would He help them?

"You are shocked, Pia. Don't you think I am capable of going against the Third Reich? God expects us to heed the laws of men until they go against His laws. I'm convinced He wants us to help His chosen people and others the Nazis call undesirable. We are in the perfect position to make a difference. Don't you agree?"

Pia licked her dry lips and nodded, mute.

"I have been thinking about this for a long while. Our tenet is to bring babies into this world. It is only God who determines who lives and who dies, but sometimes He uses us to help." *Mutti's* lip quirked. "And it won't be the first time I've given him a hand."

"What?"

Mutti patted Pia's leg. "I won't go into specifics, but over the years, before you were my assistant, I delivered babies that were labeled less than perfect, through defect or disease. Sometimes the parent wanted them done away with. Most didn't say that explicitly, but they expressed their disappointment and intentions well enough. I made arrangements for these infants to go to families who would love and care for them. My list of contacts is rusty, and it may take some time, but I believe we have it within our power to help these children disappear from under the Nazi's eyes."

"I never knew."

"There's no reason you could. I kept this aspect of my practice hidden, but you are of an age now that you should be told about the uglier side of our business. Not all parents love their babies unconditionally. Fortunately, it does not occur often, but perhaps my experience, because of these incidents, can be used for good."

"I am proud to be your daughter." Pia pressed a hand to her racing heart. "I'm still afraid, but I believe this is what God would have us do. Trudy said something to me at the market last week. I've been looking for the right time to tell you."

"You seemed to have been mulling over something this past week, but I thought it might have been the newspaper headlines. They give us much to think about."

Pia shook her head. "*Nein,* Trudy is part of a group that hides the Jews and smuggles them out of the country. They also create false papers for Jewish children, then place them with non-Jewish families. She needs our help working with the children. There are so many of them.

"Trudy wants us to house the youngsters? We don't have that kind of room. What would we tell people?"

"It would be like what you did in the past, only Trudy would tell us where the little ones are going. They would stay with us for a night or two. If anyone asks, we would say the mother had died during childbirth, or that she was ill. Trudy asked me to consider the request and pull together all my questions. I'm sure they have a system in place."

"I don't—"

"We prayed about this, *Mutti.* Perhaps this is God's answer."

A groan sounded outside the door, then pounding on the wood.

Pia leapt to her feet and opened the door.

A young woman hunched over her bulging stomach, her disheveled dark hair sticking to her sweaty, flushed face. She swayed as she gripped the wall. "Please, help me." She stumbled forward, and Pia caught her before she fell to the floor.

Mutti rushed over, and together they assisted the girl to one of the wooden chairs. Pia stayed with her while *Mutti* rushed into the bedroom to prepare for the impending birth.

Gripping her swollen belly, the girl groaned and closed her eyes. "I didn't know it would hurt this much."

"Your first?"

A nod.

"What's your name?"

The young woman's eyes flew open, terror-stricken. "Do I have to tell you?"

Pia froze. "Are you in trouble? Why can't you identify yourself?"

Tears trickled down the girl's cheeks, and her lower lip trembled. "I am Tamar." She sniffled. "And I am Jewish. Trudy said you would help me."

Chapter Six

Dieter clenched and unclenched his hand while pacing behind the shop counter. The raucous call of the cuckoo clock struck the hour. He grit his teeth. Thirty more minutes, and he could shoo away the crowd and lock the door. Any other day, he'd be thrilled to have the place filled with patrons.

But today was not any other day.

He'd agreed to help Gerhard transport two POW escapees after the shop closed under the premise of making deliveries to his customers. Secretly hauling the Allied soldiers and airmen to Switzerland was the right thing to do, but the thought did little to calm his nerves.

The clock's crawling minute hand allowed too much time to conjure up worst-case scenarios of what would happen should they be caught. Yesterday's sight of an AWOL soldier's corpse hanging from one of the lampposts gave proof to what the Nazis did to those who disobeyed. The Wallers said the young man was tired of risking his life and fled his unit. It had taken him the better part of a week to make his way home, only to be caught the following morning.

When would this travesty end?

Dieter forced a smile at the middle-aged woman who piled several cans of food and some potatoes in front of him. "Will that be all, *Frau*?"

"Yes, Dieter. I am pleased at the number of choices at this late hour."

"Excellent." He tallied the items and handed her the sales slip.

She rummaged in her handbag for coins and her ration book. "Can you figure out what I need? The information seems to change daily, and I have trouble keeping up."

"I understand." He chuckled. "I do, too."

One by one the customers came to the counter to make their purchases. His gaze bounced to the clock after each transaction. With a sigh, he rubbed his forehead. Who knew time could pass so excruciatingly slow?

"I'm sorry about your friend."

"Hm?" Dieter looked at the petite woman with snow-white curls peeking out from under a handkerchief.

"I'm sorry about your friend Gerhard. He was a nice young man."

"Was?" Dieter gasped and gripped the counter. "What happened? I didn't hear anything about him."

"He was arrested last night for hiding POWs, and this morning he was put on a train bound for Auschwitz. I thought you knew. He was your best friend."

The woman's face blurred as Dieter blinked, fighting for control. He swallowed the lump that formed in his throat. "Gerhard—" He coughed and licked his dry lips. "Gerhard would never do such a thing." How easily the lie slipped off his tongue. "He worked his farm and kept himself out of trouble."

"Perhaps he was set up, but two American soldiers were found behind a walled-off area in his barn. I heard the Gestapo got a tip and discovered them almost immediately. He didn't say anything the whole time. Mute, like a lamb to the slaughter. Tsk, tsk. Poor boy. I've known him since he was in short pants."

Dieter focused on his breathing. In. Out. In. Out. How could she be so unemotional about Gerhard? It was as if she didn't care, but that couldn't be the case. Could it? Was this harmless-looking old lady a Nazi who would rather see German lads go to their death because they believed in equality among the races and ethnic groups? He shuddered.

She patted his hand and picked up her bag of goods. "I'm sorry you had to find out about Gerhard this way. It's obviously been a shock." She glanced around the market. "I'm the last customer. You should close early and take time to recover. I'll be praying for you." Her shuffling steps scraped across the wooden floor as she walked to the door and slipped outside.

Numb, he followed her then turned the lock and flipped the closed sign. He drew down the shades then crumpled to the ground. Bowing his head, he sobbed. His cries filled the shop, echoing through the room as he railed at God.

"How could You let them take Gerhard? He was working for the cause. Were You trying to get my attention? I already agreed to help. No one survives Auschwitz. What good can possibly come of his death?"

Pounding sounded at the door, and Dieter stilled, his ears straining to catch the sound of a voice. He pulled out a handkerchief and wiped the moisture from his face and blew his nose. His heart raced. Had Gerhard released his name under torture? Was he headed for the same fate as his friend?

The knocking continued.

He called out, "Who is it?"

"A friend of a friend. Please, let me in."

"Why should I?"

"You've heard about Gerhard by now. Let me in, so we can discuss the situation."

"Go away. There's nothing to discuss."

"I'm not leaving until you let me in, and the longer I stand here shouting, the more likely the Gestapo will notice."

Dieter rose and stumbled to the door. He lifted the shade and peeked out the window. A young man with a black patch covering one eye and a jagged scar across his forehead glared at him through the glass. Another victim of the war machine.

With a grunt, Dieter unlocked the door and turned the handle.

The man shoved his way into the shop. A deep scowl darkened his face. "*Dummkopf.* You could get us both killed." He raked blunt, work-worn hands through the tangled mass of hair on his head. His mouth was a thin slash, and his face gray with fatigue.

"If you are so worried, then why did you show up at my front door in the middle of the afternoon? Who is the idiot here?" Dieter poked the man's chest. "You barge into my shop bellowing loud enough for them to hear you at the *Reichstag* without so much as identifying yourself. How do I know you aren't some sort of agent trying to get me to incriminate myself?" He shoved his hand in his pocket. "What do you say to that?"

The man heaved a sigh and sagged against the doorjamb. "You're right. In my distress, I caused panic and heartache. My apologies. Gerhard would be ashamed of me breaking under the pressure." He extended his hand. "My name is Uwe, and I am part of the team who was supposed to spirit those soldiers out of Germany. Gerhard told me you have joined us. I don't know all the details of what happened, but the initial report indicates that sometime in the middle of last night, a half-dozen Gestapo showed up at Gerhard's farm. They dragged him from the house and informed him they knew about his work against *der Führer*. The barn was torn apart, revealing the soldiers."

Uwe's voice broke. "After beating Gerhard, they loaded him and the prisoners on a train bound for Auschwitz. It left around ten o'clock this morning."

"And Gerhard's wife? His children?" Dieter's voice was barely above a whisper.

"Untouched. But of course, their hearts are crushed."

Dieter studied Uwe. "Why have you come here?"

"To ensure that you still plan to help us. We have two…uh…deliveries to be made. The…packages have been detained longer than they should have been. We must move them, and the sooner we do so, the better. You agreed to use your truck. Can we count on you, despite what happened to Gerhard?"

"He cautioned me it would be dangerous work, but I never imagined it would be worse than when I was at the front dodging bullets. On the front, you know exactly who your enemy is. At home, it is more difficult to tell." Dieter hunched his shoulders and took a wavering breath. "The woman…earlier…she said the Gestapo was told about Gerhard. Do you know who did that? Everyone loved him and his family. Who would betray him?"

Uwe shrugged. "This war has divided everyone: neighbors, friends, even family. It could have been anyone. Or no one. It seems the Gestapo needs no excuse to hunt down offenders. Sometimes, I think they enjoy attacking innocent people to see what comes of it."

"Such evil has taken over our land."

"Which is why we must band together to defeat it. Are you in?"

"Yes. Otherwise, Gerhard will have given his life for nothing."

"Good. Get your coat. We leave immediately."

Chapter Seven

Pia grabbed cans of food from the shelf and tucked them into the canvas bag hanging from her arm. She peeked over the display at the shopkeeper as he rang up items the pregnant woman at the counter selected. His crystal-blue eyes sparkled from under a thick lock of dark hair that fell over his forehead. The woman murmured something, and he threw back his head and guffawed, the somber expression on his face melting away like butter in a frying pan.

She snickered at the sound of his laughter. He glanced in her direction and dipped his head in acknowledgment. Her face warmed. She ducked and resumed shopping.

His aquiline nose and square jaw sparked a foggy memory. Where had she seen him before? Not here. This was her first visit. She'd found the shop on the way home from yet another birthing and decided to see if it had any better selection than her usual haunt. She peered at him from under her wispy bangs.

He assisted a hunched, gray-haired woman with her purchases, bending his more than two-meter frame so he was eye level with her, instead of towering above. Broad shoulders strained against the wool sweater that covered his torso. She was obviously tired today. Any other time, she'd remember where she'd run across such a handsome, considerate man.

When he gestured with his left arm, the sleeve pinned up, her eyes widened, and visions flooded into her mind. The *Rosenstrasse* protest where they'd bumped into each other. Why had he been there? She checked his attire, but no yellow star rested on his chest. He wasn't Jewish. Had he attended in support of a friend?

His missing arm suggested he'd fought in the German army, but that didn't mean he supported Hitler's cause.

"Stop staring, Pia. You're making a fool of yourself."

"I beg your pardon?" The pregnant woman stood across the aisle clutching her bag of groceries.

"What? Oh, I'm sorry. I was talking to myself. A bad habit of mine."

"Dieter is attractive, *ja*?" The woman gestured toward the shopkeeper.

"Well…" Pia fiddled with the strap on her bag.

"You don't have to answer. Your eyes say it all." A grin lit up the girl's face. "My name is Valma, and I've known Dieter for many years. My husband and I attended school with him."

"I'm Pia, a midwife. How much longer until your baby comes?"

Valma rubbed her stomach. "This little one is overdue. My *Mutti* said activity might speed up the process, so I've been walking all over Berlin. My feet are tired, but the child doesn't seem to be in a hurry."

"Babies are definitely on their own timetables. You are thin, but other than that, you look healthy, so that is good."

"Thank you. It is so difficult to obtain food. Dieter sets aside produce for me, and he brings me milk from a friend's cow, or I'd be even thinner."

"Uh, your husband, is he…away in the war?"

Uncertainty danced across Valma's face.

Pia stepped back. "Pardon the intrusion. I shouldn't have asked, but you mentioned him, so I thought—"

"My husband is away, but not with the army." Valma arched her back and rubbed it with her thumb, then glanced at Dieter who was still busy with the octogenarian. "I'm living with my *Mutti* until he…uh…can return."

"For your sake, I hope it is soon."

A tear trickled down Valma's cheek. "Me, too, but I fear that it will not be until this war is over. Perhaps later than that."

"I'm sure you already have a midwife, but should you need anything at all, please call me." Pia handed a card to Valma. "My *Mutti* and I can be reached anytime, day or night."

The young woman hesitated then took the card and tucked it in the pocket of her coat. "Thank you. I—" She dropped her bag and grabbed her stomach. Her eyes widened, and she blanched. "Oooh. Pain…" A puddle formed on the floor at her feet. "What…?"

"Your water broke. Your baby decided it was time to make an appearance." Pia wrapped her arm around Valma's shoulder. "Do you live close enough for us to get you home?"

With her eyes squeezed shut, Valma shook her head. "It is eight blocks or so."

"Too far to walk in your condition, but first babies can sometimes take a long while. Perhaps Dieter could drive you."

"But then we would have to call my midwife or the doctor. What if they don't arrive in time? I will be alone. I can't do this by myself."

The door closed, and footsteps pounded as Dieter rushed to Valma's side. "Is she okay?"

"She's in labor. We were just trying to decide whether or not she should go home."

"Why wouldn't she?"

"If the baby comes too quickly it would be difficult to move her."

Dieter frowned. "How do you know this? You are no older than she."

"I'm a midwife. I have delivered hundreds of babies." She swallowed her irritation. Why must everyone think she was too young to be a professional? "Do you have a bed in the back or some blankets? I must examine her to determine how far along she is."

"Valma?" Dieter leaned closed to her. "How long since your pains started?"

A moan, then Valma grunted. "I had some about two weeks ago, but they weren't contractions, so when I had a few this morning, I figured they were the same thing."

Relief smoothed his face as he looked at Pia. "She says they might not be real. We should get her home."

Pia cocked her head. "And how many babies have you delivered?"

"None, but—"

"Then how about you let me decide what is best for her?"

Valma sat on the floor and grabbed her knees. "Ohhhh. Are you two…going to argue…?"

"I'm sorry, Valma." Pia rubbed her forehead and looked at Dieter. "Do you have a place she can lie down other than right here?"

"But—"

"Now!"

His face reddened. "Yes, in the back. I have a bed. This way."

They stood on either side of the groaning woman and helped her to a tiny room barely big enough for the metal-framed bed and a wooden chair. A bare bulb hung from the ceiling. At least the room seemed clean. Pia had seen worse.

With a hand on Valma's back, Pia lowered her to the mattress. She removed the girl's coat and handed it to Dieter who stood frozen, his gaze fixed on the young woman's face. Pia rolled her eyes. Surely after serving in the war, he wasn't squeamish about delivering a baby. She turned her patient and lifted her legs onto the bed.

"We need some privacy for me to check her, but if she's as far along as I think, we'll need boiled water and plenty of towels. Can you do that?"

"Yes, the Wallers across the street. Hopefully, they haven't left yet."

"Excellent. Go."

"I…uh…"

"Go!"

He pivoted on his heel and clattered out of the room, footsteps fading, then the door slammed.

Pia made quick work of examining Valma, then draped the blanket over the young woman's legs. She patted her arm. "I believe you are going to be a mother before the day is over, Valma. Don't be afraid. I will help you through this."

Valma's lower lip trembled. "I don't know…" She gripped her stomach as another contraction seized her body.

"Breathe, Valma. Like this." Pia demonstrated how to take quick, openmouthed breaths. "Focus on my eyes, and breathe like that until the contraction ceases. You can do this." She grasped Valma's hand while she complied.

Moments later, Valma's grip relaxed, and she gave a tentative smile. "Did I do it the right way?"

"Wonderful. You are being very brave, which is more than we can say for your friend, Dieter."

Valma shrugged. "He's always been sensitive. I hated when he was called up to be a soldier. He must have constant nightmares because of what he saw while in combat. And he—"

A grimace marred Valma's face, and she raised pain-filled eyes to Pia.

"Breathe like last time. You're doing fine. I don't need much water, but the task will give him something to do. I should have asked him to send over *Frau* Waller."

Minutes passed. Contractions racked her body time and again.

In the distance, the door opened then closed. Rushing footsteps approached followed by shuffling ones. Dieter appeared in the doorway carrying a towel-wrapped pot, wisps of steam rising from inside. "How is she?"

Pia pointed to the chair. "Put the water over there. She's doing well. It won't be long now."

The wrinkled face of a tiny woman peered around Dieter. "May I be of assistance?"

"Absolutely. She is almost ready." Pia glanced at Dieter. "Please wait outside. And if you've a mind to, please pray for a safe delivery."

"Is there a problem?" His gaze shot to Valma's sweat-slicked face.

"*Nein.* But I take nothing for granted during a delivery."

With a curt nod, he slipped away, and Pia heaved a sigh. *Frau* Waller entered, and together they assisted Valma as her labor advanced through the afternoon.

Finally, it was time. Despite her small size, *Frau* Waller wrapped her arm around Valma's shoulder and braced the young woman as she birthed new life.

Pia eased the infant out, his cry splitting the air. *Thank You, Father. He's perfect in every way.* "It's a boy." She cut the cord, cleaned him, then swaddled his warm body in a towel. "You'll want a doctor to examine him, but he seems healthy."

"How soon before I can travel?"

"At least a week. You must recover, and he's much too young to be out in public."

"I don't have that much time. Once my midwife realizes I've given birth, she'll report it, and the authorities will come for him. I must leave."

"The authorities?"

"Valma is married to a Jew; therefore, her son is Jewish." Dieter's voice rumbled behind Pia, and she whirled to look at him. A frown creased his forehead. "The original laws were supposed to exempt their family, but now everything has changed. I tried to talk Lars and Valma into leaving when they got married." He shook his head. "No one believed it would get this bad."

"I can help." She looked from Dieter to Valma. "*Mutti* and I can get them out of the country."

Chapter Eight

Dieter gripped the steering wheel of the delivery truck as it bucked and rattled over the bomb-scarred road on the way to the Domäne Dahlem Manor. Spring was on its way, and he needed to make agreements with the farmers who worked the plots of land allocated for agricultural use after the Great War. For the second time, worldwide conflict put a halt to development plans for the property.

Although the manor was located only fourteen kilometers south of the city, the journey had taken the better part of the morning. Stopped twice at checkpoints, then stuck behind a military convoy, Dieter would be lucky to arrive by lunchtime. His stomach rumbled, reminding him he should have eaten something before starting out.

When the lush forest of *Grunewald* surrounded him, he began to look for the turn that would take him to his destination. Undamaged by aerial assaults or logging, the forest encompassed over thirty square kilometers.

Memories of hikes and camping with *Vati* brought a bittersweet smile. His father would shed his typical serious and stoic nature to don a lighthearted innocence to explore the trails among the trees. It was good *Vati* was gone—he died of a heart attack at too early an age—because he would be distraught about the direction his beloved Germany had taken.

His thoughts turned to Valma. Would he ever see her or Lars again? The enigmatic young woman who'd helped with the birth two weeks ago had spirited away his friend's wife to an undisclosed place. Pia said if he didn't know, he couldn't endanger them. A truth, but a difficult one.

A lanky man wrapped in a bedraggled coat, with a knit cap pulled low trudged along the road. The bulging canvas knapsack draped over his right shoulder swayed with his rolling limp.

Dieter pulled ahead of the man, then stopped and leaned over to open the passenger window. As the man drew abreast, he glanced inside the truck. Suspicion-filled eyes stared out beneath shaggy eyebrows.

Gesturing to the seat beside him, Dieter said, "I'm going to Domäne Dahlem. I could take you that far, if you wish."

The man continued to peer at him. "Why would you do that?"

"Because it's cold and miserable, and you carry a heavy burden."

"What do you know of my burden?" The lips in his tanned, leathery face thinned into a sneer.

Dieter shifted the truck into gear. "Suit yourself. I mean no harm." He inched the vehicle forward.

"Wait." The man cocked his head. "Why are you headed to the manor?"

"I own a small shop in Berlin and hope to make arrangements for supplying fresh produce to my customers. People in the city are tired of tinned food, and it's not sufficient. We are on the edge of starvation."

After looking up and down the road, the man gave a curt nod and opened the door. He hoisted himself into the vehicle, then dropped onto the seat with a grunt and tucked the haversack at his feet. He studied Dieter then stuck out his hand. "I'm Ingel. How'd you lose your arm?"

"My name is Dieter. During a poorly executed campaign in '41. Now, I'm only good for selling food and trinkets."

"A strapping young man like you. I find that hard to believe. Besides, providing for our people is an important job. Leaving the city to find items for your clients speaks highly of you."

"Thank you. I wish I could do more."

Ingel rubbed his thigh. "I'm going to Dahlem, too. I appreciate the ride. It's a long walk on these old legs. I've still got a piece of shrapnel from the last war, and the cold exacerbates the ache." He pointed to Dieter's empty sleeve. "With that stump you wouldn't know anything about pain, would you?"

Dieter snorted a laugh. "Seems we understand each other."

"Seems we do."

The truck rumbled as Dieter eased it forward. "Are you working one of the plots at the manor?"

"With any luck, yes. One of my friends told me some of the farmers need help preparing the ground for planting. I may be old and gimpy, but there's still life in these bones yet."

"I have no doubt. You appeared as if you could rough me up back there."

"In these days, it's best to jump to conclusions, ask questions later. Can't trust anyone." He shifted on the seat. "But I read your eyes, and I saw no guile there. After the number of years I've lived, I am a good judge of character."

"Can you read minds, too?" Dieter grinned. "Because that would come in mighty handy."

A dry, raspy chuckle wheezed in Ingel's chest. "*Nein.*" A frown wrinkled his forehead. "But it doesn't take much to figure out what those Nazi baboons are thinking. They are as subtle as an elephant in the *Tiergarten* and using Hitler's insanity to support their own evil desires."

"That kind of talk can get you executed. You should watch what you say."

"I've lived a full life and have confidence in the hereafter. Nothing can be done to this body that causes me to be afraid. In fact, there are days I wish the good Lord would take me home. I'm exhausted and greatly saddened by what has happened to my cherished Germany. I no longer want to watch as Hitler corrupts my country and deports anyone who doesn't fit his idea of the perfect Aryan. Bah! The Nuremburg laws are as ridiculous as they are dangerous."

"Dangerous, yes. But ridiculous? What do you mean?"

"Contradictory is perhaps a better word. Depending on which Nazi leader is making the decision, the result is convoluted because they interpret the law to benefit themselves. These men had designs on gaining power, and the opportunity arose as they rode on Hitler's coattails. They don't care about him. He is merely a means to an end for them."

"Two boys I grew up with were bullies, and now they are part of the SS. They do seem to take pleasure in violence."

"Exactly. Men look for ways to justify their sins, and if they can perform egregious acts in the name of the law, so much the better. And I stand by my comment that they are ridiculous. How well do you know the Nuremburg statutes?"

Dieter shrugged.

Ingel sighed. "In the interest of racial purity, German females under the age of forty-five may not be employed in Jewish households. As if young Aryan women are going to leap into bed with their Jewish employers. Such foolishness." He shook his head. "Have you read *Mein Kampf*?"

"Some, but I struggled to finish. Hitler's views are extreme and turned my stomach."

"*Ja*. Understandable, but the philosophies he expounds upon in the book are the basis for the laws. Jews may not fly the Nazi or German flags because they have been stripped of their citizenship. If they are no longer of the German nation, what gives Hitler the right to kill them? Deport them, perhaps, but exterminate them? *Nein*. Also, the government passed a law outlining the definition of who is Jewish. One is either Jewish or not. No decision based upon a law will change that."

"Why would Hitler do that?"

"Distasteful as it is, you should finish his book. He believes in what he calls Jewish Bolshevism claiming the Jews are conspiring for world domination, and as such are the mortal enemy of the German people. This coming from a man who seems intent on his own world domination."

"I didn't know about any of that. I am a simple shopkeeper."

Ingel cleared his throat. "There is nothing simple about you, friend. Of that I have no doubt. In fact, I sense you are in the midst of a difficult decision. One that involves risking your life, and perhaps the lives of those you love." He laid his hand on Dieter's arm. "One man can make a difference, Dieter. *You* can make a difference. Listen to what God is telling you."

Chapter Nine

Pia rushed down the sidewalk toward Dieter's shop, her canvas bag banging her hip. She glanced at the headlines on the stacks of *Berliner Morgenpost* and *Völkischer Beobachter* that announced the celebrations planned for Hitler's birthday. *Der Führer* would be fifty-four years old, and Berlin was going all out for the occasion.

Across the street, multicolored ribbons hung from several storefronts. Where on earth had the poor shop owners obtained such things in the midst of rationing and deprivation? The black market? Perhaps the authorities distributed the items in an effort to spruce up the city.

The late afternoon sun dipped behind the buildings. Hulking shadows created pockets of darkness. She peeked at the watch pinned to her coat and picked up the pace. A stitch knifed her side as she fought to take a deep breath.

Making the rounds to her patients had taken longer than anticipated, and now she might not make it to Dieter's before he closed. Then she would miss seeing his face light up and hear his gentle welcome. Her face warmed, and her heart skipped. Neither action had anything to do with her speed.

What nonsense. He'd not given any indication he'd noticed her, let alone felt anything more than respect for her participation in the Resistance. He'd commented twice about her bravery. Didn't he realize the level of her fear? He was the one to be lauded by hiding the Jews and other escapees in his truck and driving them to freedom.

Another group was scheduled to leave tonight. She must get the supplies to them now, or it would be too late. Hitching the bag over her shoulder, she hunched into her coat against the frigid temperature and began to run. Prickly needles of wind brought tears to her eyes, and she swiped them away to clear her vision. Only three more blocks to go.

The air-raid siren shrieked.

Her gaze shot to the cloudless sky. Of course the Allies would attack. They wanted to commemorate Hitler's birthday, too, and the clear weather gave them the perfect opportunity.

Pedestrians bumped and jostled her as they raced to safety. Could she make it to Dieter's shop before the bombs fell?

Plane engines rumbled, melding with the sharp crack of anti-aircraft fire. She ducked and pressed herself against the stone and brick façades. Was that more dangerous than running in the open? She plugged her ears against the noise. *Please, Father, keep me safe.*

Somewhere behind her a missile struck, and the ground quavered. Pia staggered, and her fingers reached for something…anything to stabilize herself. Her palm wrapped around a railing, one of the few the Third Reich hadn't removed to melt down for war materiel.

Another explosion.

Debris showered her from above and behind. Pain bit her calf. She stumbled and cried out, then turned to look at her injury. A large glass shard protruded from her leg. Blood oozed from the wound and dribbled into her sock.

Bombs continued to fall, and blasts rocked the structures on either side of her. Where was the nearest shelter?

Think, Pia!

Unfamiliar with the neighborhood, she had to make her way to Dieter's despite the distance. She squatted under a vacant overhang. Opening her satchel, she withdrew one of the towels she always carried and tore strips from the cloth. With lips pressed together, she tugged the glass from her injury. It slipped easily from the wound, and the blood flowed. With practiced motions, she cleaned and bandaged the area, then wiped her hands on the unused towel.

Pia climbed to her feet, then rotated her ankle, testing the tightness of the bandage. Satisfied it would stay put, she took a step. A burning sensation shot up her leg, and she sucked in a breath. She needed to keep moving. It was too dangerous to stay put.

She squared her shoulders and hobbled along the pavement. One. Two. Three. Four. Counting her steps kept her mind from dwelling on her stabbing agony.

Dodging pedestrians and debris, she stumbled down the sidewalk. Tears on her cheeks, added to the chill on her face. Only one more block to go. Her leg throbbed. She stopped and bent over double trying to catch her breath. A peek at the blood-soaked bandage showed her it held fast, but stitches might be required. She pressed her lips together. She'd probably need to do it herself. After a bombing raid, the hospitals would be full of those in dire need of attention more than her.

"Pia!"

Her head whipped up.

Dieter threaded his way through the undulating crowd, his face flushed. "You were late, and then the bombs started falling. I came to find you. Are you…You're hurt! Come, take my elbow. I have a basement in the shop. We'll be safe there."

She gripped his arm and limped beside him, the warmth of his body taking away some of the chill. "Who comes outside during a raid? You could have been killed."

"I know, but the thought of you out here…possibly injured…I had to look for you, but God is good, and He led me in your direction." His lips lifted in a wry smile. "No pillar of fire, but I felt His nudge all the same."

Pia giggled. "It's daytime. It would be a cloud. Perhaps you missed it after all." She sobered up. "I'm sorry to have scolded you. I've lost too many friends. I didn't want to lose another."

His smile widened, and he reddened. "Uh…you see me as a friend? That is *gut*. We need friends in times like this." He looked overhead, where the planes filled the sky like a swarm of angry hornets. "We must hurry."

"I'm slowing you down. Leave me."

"*Nein.*" With a swift motion, he scooped her into his arms, the stump firm against her back. His stride lengthened, eating up the distance to the shop.

Her stomach fluttered as she studied his profile. Gaze intent on their destination, his lips moved in a whispered prayer for safety. *Who was this man?* "You can't carry me the rest of the way. I'm too heavy."

He glanced toward her. "You are like a feather. I carried a pack heavier than you during the war. It is better this way." His gaze faltered. "Sorry, I was forward, picking you up, but speed is of the essence."

She nodded and tucked her head under his chin, his heart beating a steady rhythm in her ear. How could he not be winded?

They arrived at the shop, and he set her down. With a steadying hand on her back, he led her inside, past the tiny office where they'd brought the infant into the world just days ago, to the basement door. She stole a glance into the room. How life had changed.

He opened a door, then flicked on the light switch. "It will be just the two of us. The men we're supposed to transport have not arrived as anticipated." Grabbing a flashlight from a nearby shelf, he clicked it on and off, then tucked it into his pocket. He gestured to the stairs and looked at her bandaged leg. "Can you negotiate the stairs?"

Suddenly shy, she nodded. "I'll do my best."

He walked down two steps then turned. "Hold fast to the railing. That should help. If you fall, I will catch you."

Her lower lip caught between her teeth, she grasped the railing with both hands. She lowered her injured leg to the next step, then followed with the good leg. The knifelike pain had subsided to a deep ache as if someone gripped her calf.

The building rocked with muffled explosions outside. Pia stumbled on the last tread and fell against Dieter. His arms came around her preventing her from crumpling to the ground. She looked up at him, hands against his chest, the texture of his wool coat rough against her palms. Time seemed to stop.

Close enough to detect tiny, yellow flecks swimming in his icy-blue irises, she nibbled the inside of her cheek. The golden-brown stubble on his jaw glinted in the light from the bare bulb, and his breath sent errant strands of her hair dancing.

His pupils expanded, and he bent toward her, the air between them crackling.

Chapter Ten

Another explosion, and dust rained down from the rafters.

Dieter shielded Pia with his good arm.

Her eyes widened, fear draining the color in her porcelain face.

She ducked her head, and he pulled her close, his breath hitching at the floral scent that clung to her silky hair. She trembled against his shoulder, and he tightened his hold around her. "This way." He led her to the steel cage he'd constructed shortly after returning home. "Not exactly regulation, but it has kept me safe thus far."

He coughed, his lungs clogged with particles. With a tug, he opened the door, and they rushed inside. He slammed the door, the latch catching with a loud click. "Hopefully, this raid won't go on much longer." Dieter gestured to a pair of wooden chairs. "Would you like to sit?"

She nodded. "Thank you." Her voice rasped, and she cleared her throat.

They seated themselves, and he turned toward her. "How is your leg? Do you need me to check the bandage?"

Her face pinked. "I can do it."

Dieter patted her arm. "I understand your reticence. We barely know each other, but safety comes before modesty. I promise to be quick."

She studied his face for a long moment, then her shoulders drooped. "You're right, and as a medical professional I know that." She scooted forward on the seat and lifted the edge of her skirt.

He squatted in front of her and examined the blood-encrusted dressing. "The cloth is dry, so I think you've stopped bleeding. Does it hurt?"

"Like I've been in a knife fight. Thank you for asking me." She smiled, and his stomach fluttered as if a flock of birds had taken flight. How long had it been since a woman looked at him with something other than pity? Who was this petite, beautiful woman? Alternately, fearful and fearsome, she was burrowing her way into his heart.

"Dieter?"

He blinked, and his face warmed. He'd been caught staring. She must think him a *dummkopf*. "*Ja*. My apologies." Dieter climbed to his feet and began to pace. "Now I know how the animals in the zoo feel. Trapped."

"Would you like me to pray for us?"

He whirled and looked at her. Could his face get any hotter? He should have thought of that. "*Ja*. I apologize for not offering to pray."

"You seem to be a man of action."

"To a fault." Dieter scoffed.

Pia tilted her head. "Not always. Your actions got us to safety. I have no complaints." She held out her hand. "Let us pray."

He grasped her warm fingers and lowered himself to the chair. Electricity from their touch shot up his arm. How could he think about praying with these sensations? Did she feel them, too? Her complexion had deepened and seemed to say yes.

"Father, we are trying to rest in You, but the bombs are frightening." Pia spoke as if God was sitting next to them. "The sense of helplessness is overwhelming. Please keep us from harm. Thank you for Dieter coming to find me. Thank you for his friendship. Please keep *Mutti* safe." Her voice broke. "I know Your plans are perfect, but I don't want to lose her. Please bring the men to us safely, and help us to get the across the border without incident. Amen."

Dieter squeezed her hand. "You are close to your mother?"

Tears trickled down her face. "Yes. We always have been, and even more so after *Vati* died when I was young, during the last war." She lifted grief-stricken eyes. "Why do men resort to killing and maiming each other to solve their differences?"

He fumbled in his back pocket for his handkerchief, then used it to mop the wetness from her cheeks. "I have asked that question many times."

Pia gasped. "How insensitive of me. I forgot about your arm."

"You did?" Dieter stared at her, his heart threatening to burst from his chest. She didn't remember he had a missing limb? He glared at the limp sleeve of his coat. There wasn't a moment he ever forgot.

"*Ja.* You are so capable. And strong." She blushed again. "You carried me for nearly a block." She laid her hand on his arm. "And resist the evil trying to take over this land."

Her touch burned through the fabric of his coat, and he fought the urge to draw her to him. Would their paths have crossed if it weren't for the war? He smiled. Perhaps something good would rise from the ashes of

Hitler's flames of madness. "Thank you for your kind words. And for your faith. I've been wrestling with trusting God. How could He allow *der Führer* to succeed? For so many innocent people to die." Dieter clenched his fist. "Then He took my wife and son. It was a night like this about a year ago. She went into labor, but the bombs were falling, and the midwife never came. We couldn't get to the hospital. There were…complications. I couldn't help Greta. The baby was stillborn, and my wife died a few hours later."

"Oh, Dieter. You poor man. No wonder you were so distraught when Valma's contractions started."

"Ja. It brought back terrible memories. I panicked. What if Valma died, too? What would I have told Lars?"

"Nein. I was there. If anything had happened, the blame would have been mine." She brightened. "But all went well, and Valma has a beautiful boy."

"Who had to be secretly taken out of Germany with his mother." Dieter blew out a loud breath and jumped up. He resumed pacing. "It's going to take several more years, but we are going to lose this war. The Allies are more powerful than Germany could ever hope to be. How many more people have to die?"

"That is for God to decide. It is hard to wait, but we are doing our part. Perhaps only saving one person at a time, but it is one who will not perish. We must do what we can and wait on Him to do the rest."

Dieter finger-combed his hair. "I'm not a patient man, Pia."

"That has become obvious to me over these last weeks." Pia grinned. "Maybe God will teach you some. As a midwife, I have had to learn to bide my time. A baby is born in its own time, and nothing I can do makes the birth occur any sooner."

"Wise words. I will try to emulate you."

"I am not always as calm as I appear." She crossed her arms. "What will happen to the people who were supposed to be transported today? Did we miss the window of opportunity?" She glanced around the room. "And my bag? What happened to the supplies I brought?"

He slapped his forehead. "Your bag is upstairs. I slung it over my shoulder when I carried you, but dropped it in the doorway when we entered the shop."

"Most of the contents were medical supplies. Hopefully, they will be okay."

"*Gut.* We will have to wait for instructions about the escapees. It would be dangerous if I reached out to anyone. I pray they survive the raid. How awful if they were safe from the Gestapo's prying eyes only to die in a bombing and miss out on the rest of their lives."

Pia narrowed her eyes. "What will you do after the war? When you are no longer performing heroic deeds for those being hunted or saving damsels in distress. What does the rest of your life look like?"

"Heroic? *Nein.* I'm doing no more than the others. But to answer your question, I find it difficult to think beyond each day. I survived my time as a soldier, but that doesn't mean I'll make it through the war. The bombings will become more frequent and more deadly as time passes and the Allies make advancements in their weapons. When I wake up in the morning and I am alive, I praise God, but I am not so arrogant as to make plans." He sighed. "What about you, Pia? What will you do after this is over?"

"I will continue my midwife practice with *Mutti*. With any luck I will find a good man who will love me, and we will raise a family." She shrugged. "But if not, I will be content. I don't need a husband to be fulfilled. Not many men would want a woman who is called out of the house at all hours of the day and night."

"Then they are not worthy of you. Your work is important, and your passion is obvious. I saw you with Valma. She and her baby are alive and well because of your skills. That is a gift not to be taken lightly."

"Thank—"

A tremendous crash sounded overhead, and the light bulb shattered plunging them in darkness.

Chapter Eleven

Pia screamed and reached out to Dieter. "Did the shop take a direct hit? Will we be able to get out?"

He wrapped his arm around her. "I don't think it was a bomb. After eighteen months on the front lines I know what they sound like. There was no accompanying whistle. Let me find the flashlight, so I can assess our situation."

She shifted, and her foot kicked the abandoned light. "Here is it." She felt on the floor until she found it, then clicked on the switch. The beam cut through the blackness, easing the tightness in her chest. Would they make it out of the basement alive?

Dieter took the flashlight and swept the shaft of light back and forth across the rafters. "No damage. Whatever happened upstairs, the floor is still intact."

The muffled cry of the all-clear signal whined.

Pia blew out a deep breath. "The raid is over. We can leave."

"Are you able to climb the stairs? I'd like to go ahead of you to ensure things are safe, but I will carry you if needed." His leaned toward her in the dim light, concern wrinkling his forehead.

She trembled at his closeness. Her leg throbbed, but her heart even more so. It was best if she didn't find herself in his arms again. "Uh…my wound aches, but I should be able to get up the stairs."

Footsteps pounded on the floor above. The door to the basement opened, and a silhouette appeared in the murky light. "Dieter! Are you down there? Are you injured?"

"Horst?"

"*Ja*. Are you okay?"

"I'm fine, but Pia hurt her leg."

"Pia?"

"Pia Hertz. She is the midwife who helped Valma. I told you about her."

"Of course. I will come down." He descended the stairs, his feet clomping on the treads. "I'm sorry to meet you under these circumstances. Do you need me to carry you?"

"No, but if I could lean on your arm, that would allow me to keep my balance."

He crooked his elbow, and she grasped his forearm. With the other hand on the railing, she limped up the stairs. Biting her lip against the pain, she swallowed a whimper. Sweat broke out on her forehead as she struggled to reach the top.

Minutes later they crossed the threshold, and her eyes widened.

Behind her, Dieter gasped.

Surrounded by shattered glass, shelving, and tinned goods, a black sedan took up the majority of the shop. Cold air from outside sent dust and debris swirling. Two Gestapo agents edged around the car and pointed to Horst. "You there. Get this man out of the vehicle."

Pia's gaze shot to the car. In the commotion, she hadn't seen the poor man whose head rested against the steering wheel.

Horst frowned. "The woman needs medical assistance."

"She can wait. This man was trying to escape. We need to take him into custody. Do you want to be arrested, too? We can arrange that."

Horst scowled. *"Nein."* He huffed a breath. "But I doubt he's in any shape to escape now."

The taller of the two agents frowned. "We are not interested in your opinion. Just get him out of the car."

"Jawohl."

Horst opened the sedan door and tugged at the man until he was upright. A gash at his hairline poured blood over much of his face. "Tell my wife, I love her." His eyes rolled back, and his head lolled to the side.

Pressing his fingers against the man's neck, Horst shook his head. "He's dead."

The agents glared at Horst, then stomped from the building, their heels grinding against the glass.

Horst rushed toward the retreating agents. "What about the car and this man?"

Without turning, one of the agents waved his hand in a dismissive gesture before disappearing around the corner.

"Do you believe that? They just left us to deal with their mess."

Dieter rubbed his face. "What do I do with a dead man? And how do I get this car out of my shop so I can make repairs, clean up the mess, and reopen for business?"

"Perhaps Pastor Biedermeyer knows someone who can help us." Horst bent and picked up a stray tin. "Meanwhile, I will pack up your inventory so the looters don't have a field day, and you take *Fraulein* Hertz to the hospital where she can be properly treated for her wounds."

"Thank you, Horst. You're a good friend." He turned toward Pia "I don't know how accessible the roads will be, but you shouldn't walk to the medical facility. My truck is parked in the back."

Mute, she nodded, then picked her way over the products strewn across the floor. She stumbled, and he braced her with his hand, the skin tingling under the warmth of his fingers.

They left the shop, and Dieter helped her into the passenger side of the truck. Once behind the wheel, he maneuvered the vehicle around a pile of debris and drove down *Torstrasse.*

She sighed and rested her head against the back of the seat. Sniffling, she wiped tears away from her face.

"Are you in pain? It may take us a while to get to the hospital."

Her eyes opened, and she looked at him. "*Nein.* I'm not normally a crybaby, but today has been rather overwhelming. I think it's beginning to catch up with me. Those Gestapo seemed more irritated to have lost their prey than about the young man who died. Although perhaps he is better off not being subjected to their methods of interrogation."

"It is only better if he's a believer and is now with his heavenly Father."

"True." She examined her hands and scowled. "I must look a sight. I cannot wait to wash off today. Do you mind taking me home? *Mutti* can stitch my leg."

"*Ja*, of course. She's a medical professional. You'll have to give me directions."

She peered out the window. "I think so. We live on one of the side streets behind Humboldt University."

———————————◆———————————

They rode in silence, the truck rumbling and rocking as Dieter avoided bricks, broken glass, and other materials. Pia periodically gave instructions where to turn.

Dieter's heart warmed at the sound of her voice. In many ways, it had been a terrible day, especially with the destruction of his shop, but time with Pia soothed his weary soul. Her gentle manner coupled with her bravery during the bombing…she was unlike any woman he'd ever met.

He glanced toward her. A tentative smile graced her lips. Should he tell her how she affected him? With the uncertainty of each day, was it unfair to express his feelings? Or was the war's unpredictability the very reason he should say something?

"Pia—"

"There's—"

They laughed, and Pia said, "You first."

"No, ladies first." He braked and gestured to the stone building on the right. "Have we arrived?"

"Yes. We have some rooms on the second floor."

He turned off the truck. "Wait there." He circled the vehicle, then opened her door. Holding out his arm, he said, "Can you manage, or do I need to lift you down?"

She blushed and grasped his outstretched hand. "I'm not a total invalid, but I would appreciate your help up the stairs." They approached the door, and she fumbled in her purse for keys. "What were you going to say before I interrupted you?"

"Ah...nothing."

"Are you sure?"

"Positive. Let's get you inside. It's nothing that can't wait."

Dieter took the keys from her and unlocked the door. They made their way inside and up the stairs. Muffled voices sounded from within one of the apartments down the hall. Then the softer tones of a woman. Pia's head whipped around. *"Mutti?"*

"What is it?"

"The voices are coming from our apartment." She limped forward and opened the door, and he hurried to catch up.

The two Gestapo agents from the shop stood over a woman on a worn couch. Her features were an older version of Pia's. A red handprint marred her cheek, and a chill swept over Dieter. Certainly, it was no coincidence they were here. This day couldn't get any worse.

A feral gleam shone from the eyes of the taller agent. *"Fraulein* Hertz, your *Mutti* was worried about you. We all were."

Pia straightened her spine, but Dieter felt her hand tremble, and gave it a reassuring squeeze.

She rushed to the couch and inspected *Frau* Hertz's face. Without turning, Pia said, "What do you want? How dare you barge into my home and treat my *Mutti* with disrespect."

Dieter gaped at her. Such talk could get her arrested. "Pia—"

The agent's eyebrow rose. "Brave words coming from such a snip of a woman. Your *Mutti* was not cooperating, but now that you are here, she is of no interest to us. We know of your activities and are here to take you in for…questioning."

"Sir, she is injured." Dieter walked to the agent, his mouth dry. "She needs medical treatment."

"Then you should have taken her to the hospital."

"Her *Mutti*—"

"Enough talk." The man grabbed Pia's arm. "She is coming with us, and if we get any more arguments, you will all be arrested. *Verstanden?*"

Dieter stared as the men hustled Pia out of the apartment. His heart bled to see her go, but he would be no good to her if he was also taken.

Her *Mutti* sobbed quietly behind him.

He was wrong. The day could definitely get worse.

Love's Belief   72

Chapter Twelve

Pia stared at the back of the driver's head. She clenched her fists and focused on using the breathing techniques she taught her patients to quell panic.

The agent next to her periodically glanced in her direction, but she wouldn't give him the satisfaction of meeting his gaze. *God, help me. I'm trying to accept that Your will for me might be death, but I'm not ready to die. If You do take me home, please look after Mutti...and Dieter.*

Remembering Dieter's crooked grin, she smiled. The time spent with him had brightened her life. At first a friend, and now...what? Somewhere in the midst of working together to thwart Hitler's plans by hiding and transporting Jewish mothers and babies, she'd fallen in love with him. Too bad she might not get the opportunity to tell him.

"You think this is funny?" The man grabbed her arm, his fingers biting through her coat. "This is serious business. We have reason to believe you are breaking the law, and we will find out the truth."

She tried to pull away from his viselike grip, but he held tight. "What laws? You have no proof and are hoping to bully me into a false confession." Where had her bravado come from? A blanket of peace settled on her shoulders. *Thank you, Father. I accept whatever happens to me.*

"Such bold words from a girl on her way to Gestapo headquarters. We'll see how brave you are after we begin our…discussion." He smirked, and his words dripped with venom. Releasing her arm, he sat back and stared out the window.

She resumed her breathing exercises. What were *Mutti* and Dieter doing? She'd seen the conflict in his eyes. Anger at her arrest coupled with resignation that anything he said or did would be rebuffed. Or worse. Have him arrested. Would he try to get her released? Were any of *Mutti's* friends in a position to help?

The vehicle slowed in front of the brick and stone Martin-Gropius-Bau, once a museum for decorative arts. The adjacent building had been taken over by Hermann Göring for his Gestapo. Leave it to the Nazis to ruin something meant for beauty.

Pia's stomach lurched, and she laid a hand against her middle.

"Not so courageous now, are you?"

She pressed her lips together. Anything she said might be twisted and used against her. Silence was her best choice.

The driver remained behind the wheel, but the man next to her opened the door and slid out. He gestured for her to follow. Pia climbed from the car, her wounded leg giving way. She fell to the ground.

He hauled her to her feet. "Get moving."

Pain shot up her calf, and the warm flow of blood on her skin told her the wound had reopened. Pia bit her lip to keep from crying out. She must not show any weakness.

In the lobby, soldiers stood at attention, their rifles gripped and ready. The uniformed woman behind the reception desk studied Pia, then her eyes went blank and face impassive. Black-coated officers strode down the hall, the sound of their heels echoing against the tile and wood.

Several turns later, the man shoved her into a sterile-looking, windowless room. She whirled around as he slammed the door. The lock clicked in finality. His muffled footsteps faded, and she froze. How long before they subjected her to the torture rumored to occur behind these walls?

Her teeth chattered despite the warmth in the room. Breathe, Pia. She dropped into the lone wooden chair and wrapped her arms around her middle. Bending over she closed her eyes. "Please give me strength for whatever comes, Father. Put the words on my lips You would have me say. You know my heart and that I would like to live, but I will honor You to the end. If you choose to allow these men to take my life, help me be a beacon to them of Your hope and love."

With a sigh, she fell silent. Memories of *Mutti* played through her mind. Working together to bring babies into the world. Worshipping side by side in church. Picnics at the *Tiergarten* and walks along the Spree.

Tears trickled down her cheeks, and she swiped them away. She bent to check her wound, and Dieter's face invaded her thoughts: the smile that lit up his face, the crease that appeared between his eyebrows when he was concentrating, the way his eyes changed color with his mood. But most important was his love for God and willingness to risk his life to do what he knew what right.

She would make him proud.

Voices sounded outside, and a key rattled in the lock.

Pia sat up, squared her shoulders, and folded her hands in her lap.

The door swung open. A bearlike man filled the doorway, his left eye covered with a patch and a puckered scar that split his eyebrow and ran down the front of his cheek. His face was flushed and shiny with sweat.

She stifled a gasp. If they were trying to frighten her, they were succeeding. *Breathe, Pia. One. Two. Three.*

He marched into the room, his face a polite mask. "Good afternoon, *Fraulein.* I apologize for your treatment thus far. We merely require information from you, then you may go."

Her heart skittered. Was he playing games with her? "I am a simple midwife. What information could I possibly have that you want?"

"Nanna Conti has concerns about your practice." He tilted his head. "You know what sticklers we are about details. It seems you may not be filing all your reports."

"Reports? Of course, I am. After each birth I attend, I submit the required paperwork. I have copies at home."

A sardonic chuckle rumbled in his chest.

The hair on the back of her neck prickled. Her palms slicked with moisture, but she refrained from wiping them on her skirt.

"If we have all of your reports, indications are your business is suffering. I'm struggling to believe that a practice so successful before the…uh…conflict could suddenly be on the brink of failure."

Pia stared at him. "With all due respect, how can you say that? This conflict, as you call it, has taken our young men. They are fighting on the front lines in every corner of the globe. The only males who remain are youngsters or the elderly, neither of whom are fathering any children. Have you thought about that?"

"You are mistaken. There are plenty of soldiers here in Berlin, and surely you are aware of the *Lebensborn* program through which Germany will remain pure. Many single women participate."

A shudder crawled up her spine. She'd heard stories about the women who chose to sleep with SS officers in order to become pregnant for *der Führer*. Housed in castles, these girls were given the best food, clothing, and medical care. The more children they had, the more important they became. Did they really think Germany cared about them?

"I see from your expression, you do not agree with our methods."

"Do you care about my opinion?" She shook her head. "Ideally, children are the result of a happy and loving marriage, not a transaction on behalf of a country."

He threw back his head and laughed.

Her skin crawled at the sound. Who was this man?

"How naïve of you." A predatory smile tugged on his lips. "Everything we do is for Germany, and if you were loyal, you would know that."

"I love Germany with all my heart."

"If that were true, you would do whatever you could for the cause."

Pia crossed her arms. "Believe what you will of me. It is obvious you have made your mind up."

He narrowed his visible eye. "We digress. You must give me the names and addresses for those babies you delivered but didn't report."

"There are none. It is as you said, my practice has shrunk."

"You're lying!" He towered over her, and she flinched. *Lord, protect me.*

The door swung open and bounced against the wall with a bang.

"*Standartenführer* Schultz, what are you doing?"

Schultz wheeled around. "*Herr* Noll!"

Pia peeked around the man's girth and gaped. Impeccably dressed in a hand-tailored suit and silk tie, Bruni's *Vati* glowered at the officer. "*Fraulein* Hertz is coming with me."

"But, *Herr* Noll—"

"Another word from you, and you'll be mining ice on the Eastern Front. *Verstanden?*"

"*Jawohl.*"

Pia scrambled to her feet before *Herr* Noll changed his mind. Ducking her head to avoid *Standartenführer* Schultz's gaze, she slipped past the hulking officer.

Herr Noll extended his elbow. "Forgive the inconvenience, *Fraulein.* Please, follow me. We have much to discuss."

Why did she suddenly feel as if she'd gone from the soup pot into the oven?

Chapter Thirteen

Dieter paced along the sidewalk in front of *Herr* Noll's historic, stone mansion. The century-old home overlooked a frost-covered lawn. Spring attempted to make itself known by pushing tiny green shoots through the soil among the garden shrubs. A large fountain graced the courtyard, and statuary stared at him from among the trees.

He pulled out his watch and glanced at the time before shoving it back into his pocket. Where was Pia? When *Herr* Noll discovered Pia had been arrested, he snarled something about certain people overreaching their authority and promised to return within the hour with her in tow.

Had *Herr* Noll run into problems getting her released? Perhaps his power did not extend as far as he claimed. Would the authorities allow her to attend Bruni who was sequestered in her room in the midst of labor? The Gestapo didn't need to know Dieter had brought Pia's *Mutti* two hours ago, and the mother-to-be was already in good hands.

Like her daughter, Pia's *Mutti,* Sabine, was a fascinating combination of strength and compassion. She had the household staff running back and forth with assignments, then she'd put Dieter to work. With the butler's help, he'd collected bedding from the closets, boiling water from the kitchen, and carted the gramophone from the parlor to the girl's bedroom along with a stack of records. *Frau* Hertz selected one of

Brahms's music. She insisted the composer's works were perfect for calming expectant mothers.

The lilting strings of the violins had certainly lightened some of Dieter's tension as he hurried from the room before she could ask him to stay. Tasks completed, he was the last person who should help bring a baby into the world. He'd nearly fainted when he thought he'd have to help Valma.

He shook his head and pulled out his watch again. How much longer must he wait for Pia?

Tires squealed.

Dieter looked down the street as a pristine Mercedes-Benz 770 rounded the corner. Its spotless black finish glistened in the sun. Favored by most of the high-ranking Nazi officials, the car screeched to a halt in front of the house. The back door popped open, and *Herr* Noll leapt out.

Normally stoic and unreadable, the man's complexion was ashen and lined, adding years to his face. He rushed around the vehicle and opened the other passenger door.

Pia's head came into view, and Dieter blew out a deep breath. "Pia."

She turned, and a smile curved her lips, erasing the haunted look she wore. What had they done to her?

"Pia, are you okay?" He ran to the car, but *Herr* Noll waved him away.

She gave Dieter a wistful look then following the man up the stairs and into the house. The door closed with a loud click.

The sedan pulled away, its engine purring. Rather than use the tradesmen's entrance in the back, Dieter trotted toward the front entrance and let himself inside.

Muffled orchestral music was mingled with a woman's cries overhead. Footsteps rushed back and forth. A door opened then closed with a bang.

What to do? He was as useless as a knife without a blade. Where was *Herr* Noll? Did he need encouragement and support? Would his mask of superiority and control be in place? Would he listen to a mere shopkeeper?

A uniformed maid appeared in the foyer. She curtsied, her eyes downcast. "*Herr* Noll would like you to join him in the library." With a sweep of her arm, she gestured toward the corridor to her left.

Dieter gulped. *Give me the right words, Father.* He nodded and followed the woman as she led him down the hall. He peeked inside the rooms as they passed. Gilt-framed oil paintings hung on walls colored in tasteful shades of gray and ivory. His knowledge of furniture was nonexistent, but he'd bet a week's worth of rations that most of the items were antiques, high quality and valuable. The surfaces gleamed in the sunlight filtering through sheer curtains.

"Here we are, sir. You may enter." The woman curtsied again and scurried away before Dieter could tell her that he was unworthy of such treatment.

He stepped into the room and froze.

Herr Noll sat in a burnished leather chair, his head in his hands and silent tears on his cheeks. He raised moisture-filled eyes to Dieter. "Thank you for joining me. Waiting alone…" He shrugged then pulled out a handkerchief and mopped his face. "I see by your expression you are surprised at my emotion. Do you have any children, *Herr* Fertig?"

Dieter shook his head. "*Nein*. My wife and son died during one of the raids."

"So you understand my fear. Although perhaps you won't be a widower for long. I noticed your response to *Fraulein* Hertz." A crooked grin appeared. "And your reddened face confirms my suspicions."

"Sir—"

"No explanation is necessary. Your secret is safe with me, although you should tell the young woman how you feel. This war makes life…uncertain. You should seize the moment." He rubbed his forehead. "*Frau* Hertz is concerned. My daughter is struggling and may not survive the birthing. Are you a praying man? Bruni needs a miracle, and I'm afraid if there is a God, he will not listen to me. My sins are too great."

"Please, sir, call me Dieter, and yes, I am a Christian." His heart beat wildly. Such an admission could put him in danger, but it seemed that was of no concern for the moment. "I believe God can perform a miracle should he choose to. I can pray on your behalf, but He will listen to you if you are truly contrite for your actions." *Father, are You really asking me to lead this man to You? Surely, there is someone else You can use.*

Dieter swallowed. His tongue stuck to the roof of his mouth as nausea threatened to overtake him.

"I thought I was doing right for my family when I joined the Nazi party. *Der Führer* and his party did good things in the beginning. A wheelbarrow full of *Reichsmarks* wouldn't buy a loaf of bread, and millions were out of work. The party improved the economy and gave

Germany a reason to be proud again." *Herr* Noll sighed. "I allowed myself to be sucked into their lies when they said the Jews were the cause of our hardship. That if we sent them away, our people would be prosperous. Before I knew it, I was a cog in their despicable machine, in tacit agreement with my silence about their foul deeds. What a fool I was. I do not deserve God's mercy."

"None of us do, sir. But He loves us and wants a relationship with us. That's why He sent His Son to die in our place. Jesus was the perfect sacrifice and is a mediator between us and God. All we have to do is ask His forgiveness, and He will save us."

Hope sparked in *Herr* Noll's eyes.

Dieter leaned forward. "I'm not promising that if you choose to follow Him he will save your daughter or her child. I am proof of that. The pain from the losses of my wife and baby is still a wound to my heart, but I know He had His reasons for allowing my family's death. You must believe in His sovereignty for yourself and receive the gift He is offering. You cannot bargain with God."

"I understand, but I'm still skeptical He will accept me."

"Have you ever read the Bible, sir?"

"I went to church as a youngster."

"Well, there is a man between those pages who is much like yourself. His name was Paul, and he started out in a great position of power. He used his authority to persecute the church and kill Christians. Then God met him on a journey, face-to-face. He struck Paul blind for three days, and cured him three days later. After those miracles, Paul traveled everywhere telling people how God had saved him from his previous life. If God can change Paul, He can do the same for you."

"Astonishing. I've never heard of him."

"We've all fallen short of God's expectations, but He wants to help us. Do you want Him to make you a new person?"

"*Ja.* And when the baby is born, we must tell my daughter about God." His face glowed. "And my staff. And my friends. But first, tell me what I must do."

Dieter grinned, and a weight lifted from his shoulders. *Thank you, Father.* "Bow your head and speak to God as if He was sitting right next to you...because He is. Tell Him that you are sorry for your past wrongs, and that you'd like to become one of His followers."

Herr Noll fell to his knees and covered his face with his hands. His lips moved as he silently prayed. Minutes passed, and he looked up with a deep sigh. The worry that had creased his forehead slipped away. He extended his hand. "Thank you for your guidance, Dieter. I owe you my life."

Dieter grasped his hand. "Welcome to the family of God, *Herr* Noll."

"Please call me, Rainar. We are brothers in the faith now."

"Yes, sir...uh, Rainar."

Footsteps sounded in the corridor, and they turned. Pia stood in the doorway, fatigue and grief engraved on her face.

Herr Noll swayed. "Bruni?"

"She's fine, sir, but the baby..." She shook her head. "He was stillborn."

A sob escaped, and *Herr* Noll gripped Dieter's arm. "My daughter must be heartbroken. May I see her?"

"Not for a few minutes. *Mutti* is preparing her for visitors."

"What can I possibly do to make this all right for her?" His lip trembled. "Oh, that I could take the grief from her."

Pia glanced at Dieter, uncertainty in her eyes.

Dieter studied her. There was something else in her glance. What was she trying to tell him?

She hesitated, then squared her shoulders. "Nothing will take away the pain of her loss, but there is a way to help your daughter and another."

Dieter snapped his fingers. Of course, Bruni could take one of the Jewish babies. The child's life would be spared, and she would have someone to raise and love as her own.

Herr Noll glanced at Dieter. "You know what she is talking about?"

"Yes, and if your daughter is willing, you could put feet to your brand new faith. How would you feel about her taking one of Hitler's undesirables, a Jewish infant?"

Love's Belief 86

Chapter Fourteen

Pia's eyes widened. Had *Herr* Noll become a follower of the one true God? She'd felt an overwhelming nudge inside to speak to him about taking Trudy's baby, but fear of the consequences almost kept her mute. She was so unsure about trusting God in this situation that stepping out in faith was terrifying. Then a look at Dieter gave her the strength to obey the small voice in her head. Would God reward her obedience with a solution for her friends?

Herr Noll wrapped his arms around himself and paced, his lips moving in silent conversation. Was he praying? Arguing with himself? She understood his conflict, and her arms ached to draw him into an embrace that told him everything would be all right. Instead, she waited, nibbling on her lower lip and sending her own entreaty heavenward.

Dieter's gaze bore into her, and she forced a smile. Such a brave man, he must not see her trepidation.

When she could stand it no longer, *Herr* Noll stopped in front of Dieter, his hand outstretched. "We must save this child from certain death. I will do what you ask of me. How should I proceed?"

Pia clamped her mouth shut as Dieter grasped the man's hand, then clapped him on the back. When had the pair grown close enough for Dieter to treat her friend's father with such familiarity? Just because he was now a Christian? She shook her head. It couldn't be that easy, could it?

She crossed her arms, letting the men work out the details. As far as she was concerned, Bruni had the final decision, but only if everyone believed this sudden transformation of her *Vati*.

His responsibilities in the Nazi government were far reaching. With the knowledge that she and Dieter were in contact with at least one Jewish family, he could have them arrested…or worse. How could he change in an instant? Was his faith real or a ploy?

Dear God, is this of You? Did I hear You correctly? Dieter seems assured that Herr Noll is now one of Your children. You saved me, so I know You can save him, too. Help my unbelief.

Dieter turned and guided *Herr* Noll toward her. "I see the doubt in your eyes, Pia, but this man is a new creation. We spoke only moments ago, and he prayed to receive Christ in his heart. Welcome your new brother into the family."

Herr Noll took her hand in his and bowed. He released her, and a frown creased his forehead. "You have every right to be skeptical, and I will let my conduct be the proof you need. From today until I leave this earth, I will do all I can to make amends for my past deeds. However, we must tread carefully with this mission. Even though I am a party member, or perhaps because I am, my actions are watched at all times. *Der Führer* trusts no one, especially those close to him." He rubbed his hands together. "You remain here and pray my daughter will see reason, even in her grief. I will go upstairs and speak with her."

He strode from the room, his footsteps muffled on the plush carpet.

Pia stared at the empty space where he'd been. *Thank you God for providing. Please forgive my doubt. Keep us all safe as we go against what Hitler dictates.*

Behind her, Dieter cleared his throat. Her face flushed. He must think her a ninny. Hands clasped, she pivoted. "Everything will work out, *ja?*"

He nodded. "I think so. You weren't here for our conversation, but *Herr* Noll was in despair about his daughter. I believe God used the opportunity to reach out to him at his lowest, as He does with many of us. We don't look up until we are on our backs. That is when we are best able to see God."

"Well said. That is certainly how God reached me. This war has made me fearful when it should have made my faith stronger." She dropped her gaze. "I'm embarrassed to admit such a thing."

Footsteps, then Dieter laced his fingers in her right hand. Her palm tingled in the warmth of his touch. "Pia, please look at me. You needn't be ashamed. We have all stumbled, perhaps me most of all."

Her head shot up. She searched his crystal-blue eyes. "You? You are the most faithful man I know. I can't believe you have doubts."

A harsh laugh, and his brow furrowed. "Then I am a good actor, because I question God all the time. What is God's plan for allowing an evil man like Hitler to succeed? For all those people to die. For soldiers to be caught up in a war they don't support, to be killed…and maimed, never to be the same again."

She reached out a tentative hand and stroked his left arm, letting her fingers travel to the end of the stump. He flinched, and she drew back. "I'm sorry. Does it hurt?"

"Nein. Not right now. Sometimes there are phantom pains or feelings. At night, I awaken because it itches, and when I reach out to scratch I realize it is gone. Then I relive the battle…and shout at God for taking my hand." He shrugged. "Then He reminds me of the Apostle Paul who had some sort of ailment that He chose not to remove, so who am I to ask?"

"You are His son. You have every right to ask." She tilted her head. "Listen to me giving advice. What do I know?"

Dieter chuckled. "We are a good pair, *ja*? It is a wonder God uses us."

She giggled, and he squeezed her fingers. Her breath hitched and tears sprang to her eyes. What was the matter with her? One minute waxing philosophical about God and His mercy, the next a puddle of emotion. She extricated her hand and walked to the window, heart pounding. Did Dieter have feelings for her? Special feelings? Or was he just being friendly and kind? She *was* a ninny. Loneliness had fabricated a relationship out of thin air. Her face flamed. How to get out of this?

"Pia? Are you okay?"

"*Ja.*" She blinked away the moisture and turned to face him. "It's been an exhausting day."

"Of course it has. How could I have already forgotten what you went through before *Herr* Noll stepped in to have you released?" He hurried toward her and wrapped her in a hug, resting his chin on the top of her head. "You must have been terrified."

She closed her eyes. Maybe he did care for her. His heart beat a steady rhythm against her cheek. "At first I could barely breathe I was so frightened. Then I prayed, and God filled me with peace. I've never had something like that happen before. It is hard to describe, and to use the word amazing seems to belittle the experience."

He stroked her back. "Well, I was terrified. I thought I'd never see you again, and that idea nearly brought me to my knees." His hand stilled. "Pia, I don't know if you can love a man like me, broken and unsure of himself, but after possibly losing you, I had to tell you how I feel…how much I love you."

Pia pulled away and searched Dieter's face. Her eyes widened at his look of joy and contentment.

He smiled. "You are unlike any woman I've ever met. Beautiful on the inside with your love of God and passion for bringing new life in to this world. You are also beautiful on the outside, and I'm a better man for having met you. We've only known each other for a few months, so perhaps you aren't ready to make a commitment. But I love you and want to spend the rest of my life taking care of you and making you happy. Would you do me the honor of becoming my wife?"

Pia extricated then put her hand to his lips. She grinned. "I've never heard you talk so much in all the time we've known each other. I love you, too. I'm not sure when it happened. It almost seems as if I've always loved you. And yes, I will marry you."

With a whoop, he picked her up and swung her around before setting her back on her feet. "She said yes!"

"Shh. We must have respect for Bruni's grief, and that of *Herr* Noll. We can tell *Mutti* later when everything has been taken care of. *Verstanden?*"

He sobered up. "*Ja,* but if my face is glowing like yours, I'm not sure how long we can keep it a secret." He kissed the tip of her nose, then lowered his mouth on hers, and she drank in the taste of him. Her arms crept around his waist, tugging him closer. Their bodies melded together.

After a moment, he pulled away, and she sighed, licking her lips. He loved her. No matter what happened over the course of the war, his love was what mattered.

"If your *Mutti* approves, I'd like to get married right away. I don't want to spend another minute away from you. It will be hard enough being separated during my…uh…deliveries, and now that *Herr* Noll is involved, *business* may pick up."

"Of course, I approve." *Mutti* stood in the doorway, a broad grin on her face. "It's about time you two figured out how you feel about each other."

Dieter's face reddened, and Pia laughed. She never could pull the wool over *Mutti's* eyes.

"And I will expedite the paperwork." *Herr* Noll entered the room. "Is tomorrow too soon?"

Pia exchanged a glance with Dieter, and he wrapped his arm around her shoulder. "Tomorrow is perfect."

The End

What did you think of *Love's Belief?*

Thank you so much for purchasing *Love's Belief*. You could have selected any number of books to read, but you chose this book.

I hope it added encouragement and exhortation to your life. If so, it would be nice if you could share this book with your family and friends by posting to Facebook (www.facebook.com) and/or Twitter (www.twitter.com).

If you enjoyed this book and found some benefit in reading it, I'd appreciate it if you could take some time to post a review on Amazon, Goodreads, Kobo, GooglePlay, Apple Books, or other book review site of your choice. Your feedback and support will help me to improve my writing craft for future projects and make this book even better.

Thank you again for your purchase.

Blessings,

Linda Shenton Matchett

Love's Belief   94

Reader's Guide

1. Pia and Sabine Hertz refused to adhere to the midwifery guidelines set for by Nanna Conti. Was there a time you felt you had to disobey rules or guidelines set at work because they went against your principles?

2. Not all German citizens agreed with Nazi ideology. The Rosenstrasse Protest was just one example of a time when everyday people stood up and voiced their disagreement at the risk of imprisonment or execution. Would you have been brave enough to participate?

3. Dieter Fertig did not agree with Nazi beliefs, yet fought in the German Army because he was drafted. Over the years, much has been made about "draft dodgers," especially those during the Vietnam era. Would you have been willing to fight for your country, despite disagreeing with the reason(s) it was at war?

4. There are several secondary characters. Are there any who stand out to you? What was it about them that attracted you to them?

5. How did you feel about the spirituality in the characters' lives? Are there specific characters whose beliefs resonate with yours?

6. Think about ways *Love's Belief* points to better things to come through Jesus Christ.

7. What lessons from this story can you apply to your own life?

Love's Belief 96

Historical Background

Dear Reader:

I hope you enjoyed *Love's Belief*, a modern retelling of the biblical story of Shiprah and Puah, two Hebrew midwives who put their lives on the line by refusing to adhere to Pharaoh's law that required them to kill Jewish baby boys at their birth. Please consider reading the original story found in the first chapter of Exodus.

Pia and her mother receive a letter from Nanna Conti, chair to the central German midwifery organization. Not much is known about her early career as a midwife, but in the 1930s she became actively involved in the NSDAP (Nazi Party). She helped establish the guidelines that monitored professional practice and was well-respected internationally for her work in improving maternal mortality rates and keeping midwifery and midwives high on the political agenda in Germany. She was even able to get legal backing for the professions, highly unusual for the time. Conti spoke at international event, including a visit to London. She was appointed the first president of the International Confederation of Midwives.

Her writings demonstrate the influence of her Nazi beliefs, anti-Semitic, and racist views. Under her guidance, midwives were to inform the Public Health Authority of any children born with disabilities or genetic diseases, which led to force sterilizations of women and even the euthanasia of people with disabilities. While she was not responsible for carrying out the acts, evidence suggests she was aware of Nazi policy and what was done with the information collected by her midwives.

Information taken from https://womenshistorynetwork.org/womens-history-month-nanna-conti-1881-1951/

For text of the Nuremburg Laws, refer to
https://en.wikipedia.org/wiki/Nuremberg_Laws

Acknowledgments

Although writing a book is a solitary task, it is not a solitary journey. There have been many who have helped and encouraged me along the way.

My parents, Richard and Jean Shenton, who presented me with my first writing tablet and encouraged me to capture my imagination with words. Thanks, Mom and Dad!

Scribes212 – my ACFW online critique group: Valerie Goree, Marcia Lahti, and the late Loretta Boyett (passed on to Glory, but never forgotten). Without your input, my writing would not be nearly as effective.

Eva Marie Everson – my mentor/instructor with Christian Writers' Guild. You took a timid, untrained student and turned her into a writer. Many thanks!

SincNE, and the folks who coordinate the Crimebake Writing Conference. I have attended many writing conferences, but without a doubt, Crimebake is one of the best. The workshops, seminars, panels, critiques, and every tiny aspect are well-executed, professional, and educational.

Special thanks to Hank Phillippi Ryan, Halle Ephron, and Roberta Isleib for your encouragement and spot-on critiques of my work.

Paula Proofreader (https://paulaproofreader.wixsite.com/home): I'm so glad I found you! My work is cleaner because of your eagle eye. Any mistakes are completely mine.

Thanks to my good friend Joanne Balzer who proofed the German references in the story. Her knowledge of her family's native language is impeccable. Any errors are my own.

Thanks to my Book Brigade who provide information, encouragement, and support.

A heartfelt thank you to my brothers, Jack Shenton and Douglas Shenton, and my sister, Susan Shenton Greger for being enthusiastic cheerleaders during my writing journey. Your support means more than you'll know.

My husband, Wes, deserves special kudos for understanding my need to write. Thank you for creating my writing room – it's perfect, and I'm thankful for it every day. Thank you for your willingness to accept a house that's a bit cluttered, laundry that's not always done, and meals on the go. I love you.

And finally, to God be the glory. I thank Him for giving me the gift of writing and the inspiration to tell stories that shine the light on His goodness and mercy.

Other Titles by this Author

Romance

Love's Rescue, Wartime Brides, Book 1

Love's Rescue, Wartime Brides, Book 2

Love Found in Sherwood Forest

On the Rails

A Love Not Forgotten (Let Love Spring Collection)

A Doctor in the House (The Hope of Christmas Collection)

Mystery

Under Fire

Murder of Convenience, Women of Courage, Book 1

Non-Fiction

WWII Word Find, Volume 1

Let's Connect!

www.LindaShentonMatchett.com

www.facebook.com/LindaShentonMatchettAuthor

www.twitter.com/lindasmatchett

www.pinterest.com/lindasmatchett

www.linkedin.com/in/authorlindamatchett

https://www.amazon.com/Linda-Shenton-Matchett/e/B01DNB54S0

Sign up for my newsletter and receive a FREE short story

https://bit.ly/2MXJFgC

Interested in more historical fiction?

Visit http://www.lindashentonmatchett.com/p/books.html

Volga Region, Russia, 1923

Chapter One

"We'll die if we don't leave this place. Pack only what you can carry." Edmund Hirsch poked his bony arms into the sleeves of his wool coat that sported more holes than Swiss cheese. A paroxysm of coughing gripped his body, the result of a mustard gas attack on his German platoon nine years ago during The Great War.

After several minutes the coughing ceased, and he mopped the sweat from his forehead with a dingy, gray handkerchief. "Be ready. We set out tomorrow at first light."

"Where will we go, *Vati*?" Five-year-old Conrad's voice trembled.

"Don't be a baby, Conrad." Older by two minutes, Conrad's twin brother, Manfred, finished tying his boot laces and jumped off the chair, his shoes clomping against the bare wood floor. His bright blue eyes blazed above his hollow cheeks.

"Hush, children." Noreen stroked Conrad's white-blond hair and met her husband's terse look with one of her own. "You heard your father. There's no time to waste."

***

Noreen yanked the zipper closed on her over-stuffed canvas satchel. Always resourceful, Edmund had attached straps to the moss-green bag so she could wear it on her back. She would also carry a suitcase in each hand. The journey promised to be arduous.

Sighing, she wiped a weary hand across her dry eyes. Even if she had any tears remaining, crying was useless. It would not make their situation less dire.

Muted voices and the occasional bump filtered through the ceiling from the boys' bedroom above. Noreen shivered and hunched into her threadbare, ruby-red sweater. An impulse purchase made during her honeymoon, the garment held more memories than warmth. Edmund insisted it brought out the roses in her cheeks.

She tossed the bulging satchel to the floor and turned her attention to the yawning luggage on the bed. Two steel pots and a fry pan nestled in the bottom of one boxy, brown suitcase between faded blue towels that had been a belated wedding present from her mother and father.

Hopefully, Edmund would find somewhere they could live in his home country with enough food to actually cook. Here, along the Volga River in Russia, the crops had failed again, and the famine was entering its second year. The decision whether to eat or plant their seed wheat had caused many families to die of starvation.

Shuffling footsteps sounded behind her. She turned as Edmund enveloped her in his arms. Nestling against his too-thin chest, she breathed in his musky scent. He bent and kissed her forehead, his black beard scraping her skin.

"You work too hard." He tucked a stray strand of her nutmeg-colored hair behind her ear.

She leaned into his touch. "Isn't that why you married me?"

"No, *Schatzi,* it is most certainly not." He grinned. "You stole my heart. I had to marry you, or I would die a broken man."

"Don't joke about that. Our friends are dying every day." She frowned. "Who knew this famine would last so long? If it weren't for the bit of help arriving from America's Volga Relief Society, matters would be much worse."

"They are sending more assistance than we are receiving. Jakob told me there is proof the government is confiscating some of the packages and keeping the money to construct new buildings and conduct repairs. As always, development of the country is valued above the lives of the people."

"Shhh!" She pressed the work-worn fingers of her right hand against his lips. "You could get in trouble for saying that. Then where would we be?"

Edmund hugged her. "There is no one to hear us, but I understand your fear. Many unexplained disappearances make for extreme caution."

He released her and gestured toward the pile of clothes on their bed. "Enough depressing talk. What can I do to help?"

"Do you have our passports? With the government ratcheting up the price, we have no more savings to purchase new ones."

"Now who's speaking out against the authorities?" He patted the breast pocket of his coat. "I have the passports and our traveling papers safe and sound."

"Good." Noreen waved him away. "Then go see what the boys are about. I gave explicit instructions about what to pack, but they have a mind of their own." She shook her head. "Well, Manfred does. Conrad simply tags along."

He kissed the tip of her nose and raised his hand in mock salute. "*Jawohl!*"

She giggled and pushed him out of the room. Closing the door behind him, she sobered and dropped to her knees next to the bed. "Dear Heavenly Father, thank You for Edmund. He is a good man. Give him strength for the journey and keep us safe as we travel. Soften the hearts of his family so they will welcome us home."

Home.

Berlin was Edmund's home. Not hers.

English born and bred, Noreen stroked the floral bedspread as visions of daffodils in Regents Park flitted through her head, their golden yellow blooms swaying in the breeze. Big Ben soaring into the sky. Tower

Bridge spanning the River Thames. Pristine white swans fishing the waters of Serpentine Lake in Hyde Park where a chance meeting changed the trajectory of her life.

In an effort to heal his damaged lungs, Edmund moved to London after the war. Someone told him the damp English air would act as a balm. A lover of art, he had attended the Spring Festival where she sat under a tent selling her baskets.

She climbed to her feet, and her gaze sought out the willow basket on their dresser. The basket Edmund purchased when he returned to her booth after taking his girlfriend home. His last date with the woman.

Noreen's smile broadened. Who knew basket weaving would catch her a husband? She flushed as she remembered the conversation.

"If I purchase this basket, will you go out with me?"

"What about your girlfriend?"

"I told her we were finished, that I was going to marry you."

"Isn't that a bit rash? You don't even know me."

"I know enough."

After a whirlwind courtship, Edmund asked for her hand in marriage. Her parents objected, so Edmund took her to the register office where he wed her in front of two gray-haired, bored-looking clerks. A year later the twins were born, and her parents decided being grandparents was more important than holding a grudge. They eventually grew to love their German son-in-law as much as their daughter did. Enough to support the family's move to Russia in another effort to heal Edmund's lungs. She swallowed against the lump in her throat. Her parents' death last year in a train accident still stung.

Overheard, a thump followed by laughter broke her reverie. Warmth filled her. She loved her country, but she loved Edmund more. That is why she would leave all but her most necessary possessions and travel to yet another foreign country to live with her in-laws. People she had never met who spoke a language she didn't know.

www.ingramcontent.com/pod-product-compliance
Lightning Source LLC
Chambersburg PA
CBHW021025120726
47905CB00009B/3176